THE LITTLE SNAKE

A.L. KENNEDY

CANONGATE

This paperback edition published in 2019 by Canongate Books

First published in Great Britain, the USA and Canada in 2018 by
Canongate Books Ltd, 14 High Street, Edinburgh EH1 1TE

canongate.co.uk

Distributed in the USA by Publishers Group West and in Canada by
Publishers Group Canada

First published in Germany in 2016 by Karl Rauch Verlag
GmbH & Co. KG, Düsseldorf

1

British Library Cataloguing-in-Publication Data
A catalogue record for this book is available on
request from the British Library

ISBN 978 1 78689 387 1

Typeset in Centaur MT by
Palimpsest Book Production Ltd,
Falkirk, Stirlingshire

Printed and bound in Great Britain by
Clays Ltd, Elcograf S.p.A.

THE LITTLE SNAKE

'A miniature fable . . . In this bitter age of broken borders, this timely, timeless story's large helping of sugar is not unwelcome'
Sunday Times

'An urgent reminder of the small and great things that actually give life its meaning'
Financial Times

'[A] moving tale about the friendship between a young girl and a magical snake, with a serious message to impart about power, wealth and war'
Evening Times

'Playful . . . sweet, sad but always a hairsbreadth away from whimsy, it's told in a soothing tone that, for better or worse, makes you feel as if you're sitting cross-legged on a classroom carpet'
Daily Mail

'Kennedy offers a gentle, clear-sighted and deeply moving commentary on what humanity really means'
Scotsman

Also by A.L. Kennedy

Novels
Looking for the Possible Dance
So I Am Glad
Everything You Need
Paradise
Day
The Blue Book
Doctor Who: The Drosten's Curse
Serious Sweet

Short story collections
Night Geometry and the Garscadden Trains
Now That You're Back
Tea and Biscuits
Original Bliss
Indelible Acts
What Becomes
All the Rage

Non-fiction
The Life and Death of Colonel Blimp
On Bullfighting
On Writing

Children's books
*Uncle Shawn and Bill and the Almost Entirely
Unplanned Adventure*
*Uncle Shawn and Bill and the Pajimminy-Crimminy
Unusual Adventure*

For V.D.B

This is almost, but not quite, the whole of the story about a remarkable, wise little girl. She was called Mary. Everything I will tell you here began when Mary went walking in her garden on one particular afternoon.

Mary was a little bit taller than the other girls her age and had brownish crinkly hair. She was quite thin, because she didn't always have exactly enough to eat. She liked honey and whistling and the colour blue and finding out.

She lived in a city filled with very many different kinds of people. Its very many different kinds of people made it a very wonderful place, full of interesting songs and stories, foods and clothes and conversations. Nevertheless, the people in charge of the city were not overly fond of people and so some of the apartments in which the very many different kinds of people lived were often dry where they should have been wet, or wet where they should have been dry, or just cold and dark and supplied with especially listless electricity. In order to enjoy the sky, which was free to them and as large as can be, the people in the wet and dry houses would fly kites from their roofs. Some looked like birds of paradise, some looked like fish and some looked like wonderful serpents.

Other houses – like the ones owned by the people who ran the city – were luxurious and stretched into the sky with great towers much higher than the kites. These apartments contained beautiful pools to swim in, or to keep fish, or perhaps vast tanks containing large reptiles like crocodiles and blue iguanas. And they had larders as big as living-rooms and living-rooms as big as meadows and probably meadows in their basements that were as big as small counties with jewelled rollercoasters and golf courses made of cake.

Mary knew about all this. She knew about all kinds of things and was very clever. Standing in her garden – which was on a rooftop and a bit bigger than a big tablecloth – she could look one way and see the very many sad, tiny houses of the squashed-in people. If she looked the other way, she could see the tall, sparkling buildings full of crocodiles and meadows.

The building where she lived was only a little bit squashed. And its pipes only leaked on Mondays and Wednesdays and at weekends, and when they did her mother would put metal basins under the drips and the metal would ring like small bells – or maybe more exactly like small, wet bells – when the water hit them.

Mary's flat was just the right size for her mother and her father and herself – which was all there was. Sometimes she wanted a little brother or sister to play with, but then she would remember that a little sister might get jealous of her cleverness, or be interested in ballet dancing which would be noisy, or wood-carving which would be messy. Mary was sleeping in a bedroom that was supposed to be a store cupboard and if she had to share it with a sister then it would seem crowded. And maybe her new sister would snore, or have very long and pokey feet.

A little brother might eventually grow up and stop lying in his baby crib wriggling his fingers and might want to run about – and their garden was too small for running about. The people who were in charge of the city and who didn't very much like people hadn't made many parks for children to play in, or for adults to sit down in and eat ice cream and tell each other how wonderful their children were (or how terrible their children were, depending). Mary thought the people who ran the city probably weren't interested in parks, because they could enjoy their own waterfalls and perhaps swim with their own crocodiles and make treehouses and swings in the thick rooftop forests she could see if she stared very hard all the way from her garden up to the shining towers.

People who came to visit the city would talk about it in the way that adults do in front of children, saying just what came into their heads and imagining that someone as small as Mary would not be able to understand them, or pay attention. They would say, 'This city is very interesting, but there are no flowers to smell here and that makes us tired.' Or they would say, 'Things here are very expensive and we cannot afford to buy tickets so that we can hear people sing, or listen to music and dance. And we are surprised by the price of large sandwiches.' Or else they would say things like, 'This city seems to want birds and not people. It is covered in edges and ledges and nooks and crooks for birds to enjoy and is full of food scraps that are small enough for beaks. It was built by people, but it would prefer birds.' And this is often true of cities. They need people to build them, but they prefer birds. This can make them sad places.

Mary thought that the visitors should come and have dinner with her parents and sniff in the nice

4

scents of soup — or maybe go and stand in her little garden and smell the roses in it. Or they could talk to the lady in the bread shop, who whistled and hummed while she fed the birds with breadcrumbs and also fed the people with bread because she liked both birds and people. Or they could watch the beautiful dancing of the kites. Or they could listen to the gentleman who sang almost all day on Sundays and who lived across Mary's street and who wore a vest instead of his shirt in summer. Any sensible and observant visitor would then see that they were in a friendly city filled with good things and happiness.

Mary liked the city and her garden. She could walk across the garden in six steps and walk from its top to its bottom in eight steps. On some afternoons she would take very tiny paces and this would allow the garden to seem twice the size and much more beautiful. The grown-ups she explained this to became confused.

They would tell her, 'The garden is the same size, no matter how many paces you squeeze into it.'

She would tell them, 'Not at all. The longer I take to cross the garden, the larger and more extremely wonderful it becomes, in the same way that ice cream becomes much more magnificent when you eat it very slowly with a little spoon.' As I said, the girl was very clever.

5

'Then your ice cream will melt,' said the grown-ups.

And Mary would shake her head and start to skip and hum a tune to herself, because grown-ups expect children to do such things and it pleases them much more than questions they can't answer. She did not mention that if she stood perfectly still in her garden then it went on for ever, because she could never reach its end. That would have made the grown-ups frown.

This – as it happened – made the grown-ups the exact opposite of the little girl.

Anyway, as I said at the beginning, if you remember, this little girl called Mary was one day walking in her garden. She believed it was hers because she loved it. She believed that loving something should make it a part of you, in the way that your feet are a part of you. (And you would, of course, be very foolish not to love your feet – should you have any – because they can be quite useful.)

On this particular afternoon, which was a wintry Sunday, the girl was taking extra-tiny steps so that her garden stretched for miles, almost into other countries. This made the four rose bushes into four giant rose trees and the three flowerbeds into vast prairies and the tiny pond into an inland sea of impressive dimensions. Sadly, it still had no crocodiles.

The little girl put her hands in her pockets to keep them warm because she preferred this to wearing gloves. This was definitely not because she had lost her gloves, as her mother had suggested earlier. The girl also watched her breath appearing in ascending, steamy clouds, as if her body were somehow burning the dead leaves from autumn, or perhaps washing a large number of sheets and producing steam like a laundry. She was perfectly absorbed by what she was doing and so it took a while for her to notice that one of her ankles was feeling slightly unlike the other.

When she looked down to her left she saw that, snugly fitted around her neatly darned woollen stocking, a golden bangle had appeared. There were two jewels in the bangle that glittered, and from time to time the bangle itself seemed to shimmer, almost as if it were moving.

It was immensely handsome.

She knew this because it told her so. Because she was very sensible, the little girl had not yet acquired the silly habit of talking only to people and would happily address objects and animals that seemed to be in need of conversation or company. 'Good heavens,' she said to the bangle. And then, 'Where did you come from?' And after that, 'Hello.'

'Hello,' replied the bangle. 'I am immensely hand-some.'

'Oh,' said the girl. 'Hello, Mr Handsome.'

The bangle rippled round her ankle and glistened and its two jewels gleamed like two pieces of jet or perhaps very dark rubies. 'No, no. I am not called Immensely Handsome – that is just one of my many qualities. I am handsome, wise and agile. I also have a beautiful speaking voice. And I am extremely fast.'

At this point Mary thought that the bangle was also rather boastful and she interrupted it, even though it did have a very lovely speaking voice.

'What is your name, then? And you don't seem that fast to me.'

'Oh, don't I . . . ?' And at once the bangle disap-peared.

It moved so quickly that Mary was still listening to its delightful voice, chuckling to itself and left behind, while its body had gone somewhere further away. She had to search about before she saw the bangle hanging from one of the rose bushes' branches. 'Maybe you shouldn't do that – the rose might not like it.'

'Oh, the rose won't mind me,' said the bangle, grinning a tiny grin and swaying slightly. 'I am the fastest thing you will ever meet,' the bangle confided, once again right there on her ankle and not even slightly out of breath.

'That is impressive,' admitted Mary.

'I know.'

'But what is your name?'

'Maybe I will tell you in a while. You should always be careful about giving your name to anyone and not do it straight away.'

'Well, if you won't tell me your name, what kind of bracelet are you?' Mary sat down very carefully under one of the rose bushes to look more closely at her talkative new friend.

'I'm not.' The bangle unfastened itself and — quickly, but not so quickly that Mary couldn't watch — shifted its golden shape along until it was wound around her wrist a few times as if it were a bracelet after all.

'Ah,' Mary said, 'I see.'

The bangle slid and wriggled and tickled until she was cupping most of it, neatly coiled in her palm, and the two flecks of colour which she had thought of as jewels were looking at her from a slender, gilded head.

The red jewels blinked like clever, tiny eyes. This was because they *were* clever, tiny eyes.

'Yes,' said the snake, 'I am a snake.' And he smiled

for an instant as much as someone can with no lips and flickered out an elegant bright red tongue that was forked at the end and licked the air around it. 'You taste of sweets and soap and being good.'

Mary stuck out her own tongue, but couldn't taste anything about the snake.

'I taste of nothing,' the snake told her. 'Aren't you afraid? People usually are afraid of snakes. When they see me they frequently run up and down and wave their arms and scream.'

'Would you like me to do that?'

'Not especially,' purred the snake. 'But shouldn't you be terribly afraid?'

'Why? Are you terribly frightening?'

The snake waggled his tongue and sampled the air again. 'Well, I could be . . . Snakes can be incredibly dangerous. Some of us crush large animals in our muscular convolutions and slowly swallow whole crocodiles, or maybe canoes, or canoes with people in them.'

'But you're only small.'

'I can get bigger.'

Mary thought this might be a lie, but she didn't want to hurt the snake's feelings.

The snake stretched up his little spine and raised his small head so that he could look straight at her.

He swayed his neck back and forth as if he were listening to music and stared into her blue eyes with his dark red eyes and his strange narrow pupils which were blacker than the back of a raven and which seemed to go on for ever if you concentrated on them and really paid attention. 'Some snakes can bite you once and fill you with enough poison to kill twenty men, fifty men, maybe even a hundred men.'

'I'm not a man,' said Mary. 'I'm a little girl.'

The snake blinked. 'You are being difficult. A snake could poison you even faster than a man because the poison would have less far to travel.'

Mary nodded. 'I know. Although I think even a very huge and ferocious snake might not kill a hundred men.'

'Definitely at least twenty.' The snake sounded slightly cross.

'But I have learned all the poisonous snakes and their stripes and their habits in case I travel to faraway lands and have adventures when I am older. Your kind of snake is not in any of my books about snakes. And I have read a lot.'

This was true – Mary had read a great many books about snakes. She had borrowed them from the library and taken notes.

'Some snakes have feathers and drink the blood of warriors and some live in the Underworld in Egypt. And others darken the sun when they fly and crack their tails like thunder,' boasted the snake.

'That sounds like stories about snakes, not real snakes at all. And the last one seems more like a dragon than a snake. Dragons are in the books of things that don't exist,' said Mary sternly.

The snake sighed and lowered himself to lounge in her hand, suddenly seeming as soft as a piece of silky rope. 'Oh, well . . . Perhaps I seem less impressive than usual because I am hungry. Would you happen to have a mouse that I could eat?' The snake's head lolled off her palm as if he were almost faint with hunger, but his eyes watched her carefully and glowed.

'If I did have a mouse, it would be my pet mouse and I wouldn't ever give it to anyone so they could eat it.'

'But I suppose that you eat fried fishes and grilled cutlets of lambs and stews of cow pieces and goose's legs . . .' He lolled again, wheezing as if he were famished.

'Well, yes, but I had never met the lambs and cows and geese,' explained Mary. 'It would be rude to eat somebody I had met. And mostly we eat stews with vegetables and beans and things which don't cost as much as meat. And we're very far away from the sea here, so we don't eat very many fishes. Do you live in a jungle?'

'No.'

'I would love to know what a jungle is really like.'

'Your mind is wandering. I am very hungry.'

'Tomorrow — which is Monday — we have sewing lessons at school. Mrs Kohlhoffer who teaches sewing always says my mind wanders. She doesn't understand that I already know enough about sewing for the rest of my life. I am not going to embroider little covers for the backs of chairs ever again. I shall not embellish more slippers, or sew another bag to keep my sewing things in. I am not even going to be a surgeon — which would mean I had to sew my patients back together once I had sliced them open. No surgeon would be very popular if she embroidered flowers on her patient's operation scars. I am going to explore the world and maybe a lion will bite off my leg, or an arm, or something, or I will need to sew up a wound caused by a machete — but I already know the right stitches for wounds, and for making tidy stumps after amputations.'

The snake was sitting up again — if we can describe a snake as sitting up — because he was interested in

Mary and had forgotten that he was pretending to be hungry. 'Little girl, little girl, the world is an odd place to explore and you must promise me,' he said in his wonderful voice, 'that you will be extremely careful wherever you go.'

This seemed a kind thing to say and so Mary gave her name to the snake. 'I'm Mary.'

'Thank you, Mary. Mary . . .' said the snake in a voice that sounded as if he were thinking of something sweet and sad. 'Well, Mary, I have been in the jungle at times and I know that when you are there you must always keep your machete very sharp so that it cuts easily and smoothly and safely. And put it back tidily in its sheath when you aren't using it and never annoy a lion so much that it wants to bite you. In fact, avoid lions and all large cats. And also bears. And definitely hippopotamuses.'

'I thought you were weak with hunger.'

'I am worried about you. But you are also full of remarkable wisdom – you should write down the things I tell you so you won't forget.' The snake blinked. 'But, yes, I am very hungry, too. Do you have, at least, some cheese? I might be able to survive on cheese. A little Gruyère, perhaps?'

Mary leaned in very close and kissed the snake on its nose. (Although, of course, it didn't quite have a nose.)

'You are very forward,' the snake mumbled. But he also – like poured gold – slipped himself around and around her arm in a pleased way that sparkled his scales delightfully. Then he came to rest peaceably in her hand again. 'You maybe could call me Camatayon, or Bas, or Lanmo, or . . .'

Because the snake seemed to have a great many names and because Mary liked the sound of that one she told him, 'Lanmo. I will call you Lanmo.'

'Yes, that will be good.' The snake nodded.

'Thank you for your name.' Mary realised she was a little bit hungry herself. 'Shall we go indoors? I can toast some cheese on bread. I know how to toast cheese.'

The snake angled his head as if he were thinking. 'I think I would have to have cold cheese with no bread – because of my teeth. Toasted cheese would be too sticky.' He opened his dark mouth carefully and slowly so that Mary could see his teeth, which were as white as bones and pointed. To the left and to the right of his front teeth he had a longer fang that was most especially pointed.

'Goodness.'

'I eeth ill oh ur oooh,' said Lanmo the snake.

'I beg your pardon?' Mary had been taught to be polite.

Lanmo closed his mouth and his needly teeth fitted together perfectly for an instant, before he tried again to speak. 'My teeth will not hurt you.'

'Oh.'

'I promise.'

'And what kind of snake are you?'

'The kind that is never in books.' And he nuzzled his head against the back of her hand and flickered his tongue.

Mary did find the snake some little pieces of cheese and he ate them daintily before telling her thank you and disappearing in his fast and snaky way.

This made Mary feel a little lonely for the rest of the afternoon, until she was eating her own dinner that evening – which was vegetable stew and then more vegetable stew – and noticed that the glow of two red eyes was blinking out from under her napkin.

'Oh,' she said out loud and then, because her mother and father had turned to look at her, she had to continue. 'What lovely stew. Yes. Oh. What lovely stew.' She did this because she realised that her parents might well wave their arms about and scream a lot if she said out loud, 'Oh, I have a beautiful snake called Lanmo under my napkin. He has come back to see me again and so maybe he is going to be my friend.'

Lanmo, faster than a silky whisper, slipped into

the pocket of her dress and she could feel him moving very slightly in a way that might mean he was giggling. This made her smile and she had to turn her smile into one that looked as if it could be about stews and not snakes.

Later, when Mary was by herself in the bathroom, getting ready for bed, she looked in her pocket, but there was no one there. Lanmo had gone again. She guessed, correctly, that he had done this so she could change into her pyjamas and brush her teeth in private. When she opened her bedroom door, there was the snake, curled on her pillow, tasting the air with his forked tongue and looking at her with his sharp red eyes. They shone in the tiny, dim room, which had no window because it was really a cupboard. He was trying to look domestic. 'Hello, Mary. I am going to watch over you until you are asleep. I will keep away your nightmares.'

'But I don't have nightmares.'

'You might now – you have a snake on your pillow.' Lanmo grinned and rippled over so that Mary could get into bed and be snug. Then he lay very flat on top of her covers so that he could look into her eyes. 'You will always be safe when I am here. Because I am your friend and I will come and visit you many, many times.'

'Good,' said Mary into her blankets, because she

was very drowsy. She thought that Lanmo's eyes reminded her of sunsets and somehow this made her very really extremely sleepy.

And the snake watched her until he knew she was dreaming safely and then he told her again, 'I will visit you many, many times.' He nodded his head sadly. 'And then I will visit you one time more.' He licked the air to be sure that she was happy and he tasted truth and bravery and toothpaste and soap that smelled of flowers and it made him sneeze one short, snake sneeze. '*Pffs.*' And he could taste that in her dream she was already canoeing down a mighty river that wound between tall jungle trees with a pet lion at her feet. He felt a little jealous that she wasn't imagining him with her in the canoe.

But then again, the snake was not any kind of pet.

Once Mary was fast asleep, the snake travelled invisibly and quicker than a thought across the city until he was in the basement of a man called Mr Meininger. The basement stretched away for miles in many directions. It was the most magnificent and impressive of all the city's millionaire caverns and had taken two hundred imported Bolivian miners a year to excavate. It had a lake for swimming, although Mr Meininger couldn't swim, and it had many ice cream machines, although Mr Meininger didn't like ice cream. It had wonderful statues and fountains, although Mr Meininger wasn't especially interested in art or in dancing water. It had an orchard that was supplied with electric light so the apples and plums and peaches planted in it had to grow all the time and could never rest in darkness. They could never feel the little feet of animals, or birds, or insects tickling them, because no living things were allowed in the basement without Mr Meininger's permission. He had only ever given his permission to the two hundred imported Bolivian miners, the trees, his many servants and the tumblers and comedians he sometimes paid to try to make him smile.

He didn't smile. He thought it was a foolish waste of effort and almost as stupid as wanting to make someone else smile. He also thought it was a good punishment for the tumblers and comedians if they had to keep on balancing and falling and doing tricks and telling him funny stories and jokes while he stared at them like a giant, solemn frog in a big silk dressing gown. He made them keep on and on until they cried, and if they didn't cry he refused to pay them.

All this meant that Mr Meininger was both surprised and irritated when he looked up from reading a report on how fast his wealth was growing and saw the face of our friend the snake.

I think we can call him our friend, because we are surely Mary's friends and her friends must therefore be our friends, as long as they are nice and kind.

'Ugh,' said Mr Meininger. (He was too fat to wave his arms about and too dignified to scream.) 'A snake.'

'I know,' said the snake and flickered his tongue and slipped around the sleeve of Mr Meininger's dressing gown like a gold braid decoration – except with teeth.

'Ugh,' said Mr Meininger. 'A talking snake.'

The snake blinked. 'I know that, too.' He angled his head to one side, as if he were studying Mr Meininger very hard indeed. 'Now, perhaps you could tell me something I don't know.'

Mr Meininger was used to being surrounded by extremely respectful servants and sad, exhausted trees. When he met people beyond his cavern they were deferential and gave him gifts, because you will always be given gifts if you already have too much. And if he wasn't bowed to and petted and coddled he would usually go very red in the face and bellow, or go very white in the face and growl that everyone should be fired at once. And everyone would be. This happened even if the people being fired were prime ministers, film stars or kings. Mr Meininger practised his growl sometimes when he was in the bathroom and would look at himself in the mirror to make sure he had perfected his chilling stare. An unauthorised animal in his cavern would usually have been the cause of bellows and stares and all kinds of redundancies. But Mr Meininger couldn't say a word and it seemed to him that his skin was becoming clammy and too tight.

'Well . . . ?' asked the snake and waited politely.

And even though the snake's voice was like buttered velvet and even though the snake was being very quiet and courteous, Mr Meininger found that he was very frightened of that sleek golden body and that delicate golden head.

'I have come a long way to meet you,' said the snake. His tongue tested the air and allowed him to taste Mr Meininger's cramped, dark thoughts and his shallow, dim heart and his calculating brain. He could also taste fear that was thick as fog. 'You might at least tell me your name.'

And Mr Meininger couldn't help but say, 'Karl Otto Meininger'. If you had been there to hear him you would have noticed he sounded as if he were answering a schoolteacher or filling in a form. Then he blurted out, 'I am the third wealthiest man in the world.' He mentioned this because it had always impressed people before, although he already felt that he knew the snake was not people and would not be impressed.

'No,' the snake murmured in his sweetest voice. 'You are only the fourth wealthiest. Ten minutes ago the copper mines of Lembit Quartak made him the third wealthiest.' The snake eased higher up Karl's sleeve. (We can call Mr Meininger Karl, now that he has told us his name.) Lanmo's body came to rest on Karl's left shoulder and he whispered, 'And it really doesn't matter, anyway. It never did.'

Karl swallowed while the gentle breath of the snake pressed against his neck. 'Please.' Karl hadn't said please for years and years – there had been no one he'd thought it was worth saying to.

'Please what?' asked the snake and the question made Karl's skin shiver from head to foot. 'What would you like, Karl Otto Meininger, who is the fourth wealthiest man in the world?'

'Please don't.'

'Hmmm.' The snake slipped around the back of Karl's neck and came to rest on his other shoulder. He breathed into Karl's right ear. 'I think I can taste how many times other people have said that to you and how many times you have ignored them.'

'I didn't mean it.'

'Of course you did,' purred the snake. 'You can be

honest with me. You might as well. You ignored them every time, didn't you?'

Karl made a kind of garckling noise that he recalled other people making when he forced them to work all night on their children's birthdays, or fired them the day before Christmas, or decided to knock down their homes just to prove he could. Then he said, 'I'll give you everything I have.' Other people had told him that, too.

The snake rubbed his head against Karl's ear and Karl heard the rustle of immaculate scales. 'I cannot take everything you have.' The snake paused. '. . . I will only take everything you are.'

And then the snake opened his beautiful mouth and his tiny needle teeth shone white as bone.

In the morning Mary woke up early and discovered that she felt more rested and cosy than she ever had before. When she rolled on to her side there was Lanmo coiled on her pillow. He may or may not have been sleeping, but certainly his eyes were closed and he was making small *th-th-th* noises which might have been the way that a snake snores. Mary smiled at him and kissed the smooth, warm top of his head where it glimmered in the dull light of an autumn dawn which was shuffling in around the closed door. 'Good morning, Lanmo.'

The snake – who was in fact perfectly awake – opened his ruby eyes and licked the end of Mary's nose to make her laugh. 'Good morning, Mary. Did you sleep better and deeper than you ever have?' Then he sleeked along the blanket and wriggled and tied himself in knots and untangled himself out very straight and then curled his body into a nice curve and raised his head. 'That is how a snake wakes up,' he explained. 'If you ever see another snake doing that do not interrupt her, or him. In fact . . . do not have anything to do with snakes who are not me. One never knows.'

'What if I see a very lovely snake?' asked Mary, teasing.

'There are no snakes lovelier than me,' said Lanmo firmly. 'May I have some more cheese for breakfast? I am tired.'

'Didn't you sleep well?'

'Not really.'

M ary did sneak a nubbin of cheese out of the larder for the snake and fed him while he rode on the top of her satchel, peering about over her shoulder as she walked along in the frosty air, all the way to school.

'Snakes do not go to school. Everything important in the world is written on the inside of our eggs. When we have finished reading and memorising what is written, we break our eggs and hatch.'

'Really?' said Mary as she strolled across the playground, feeling much less lonely than usual.

'Perhaps,' said the snake, looking absolutely just like a snake and licking the interesting air very quickly, because it had so much to tell him. Several teachers looked straight at Lanmo, but because a small girl never does have a golden snake calmly reclining on her satchel they assumed that they were looking at a strange kind of handle, or that their glasses were dirty, or that they were mistaken. None of the children spotted the snake, because they were busy with each other and, as usual, had no time for Mary.

While Mary sat in a number of classrooms and learned about the colours of money and the lengths of different silences and the average weights of heights, the snake nipped and slipped from classroom to classroom and explored.

The snake found the school very odd. In one room the teacher was telling the class, 'You will see on the board all of the answers for today's National Test. You will spend this period copying down the answers on to your National Test Papers. If you have copied down the answers correctly you will then be clever enough to take next week's National Test.'

A small boy with ginger hair who sat at the back of the classroom put up his hand and asked, 'But shouldn't we be learning things like why the wind blows and which way is up and how to tie our shoelaces and what is love?'

'No,' said the teacher. 'We should be proving that we are clever so that the National Test Assessors can assess us, and when we have been assessed we can move on to our next assessment.'

The small boy with ginger hair – his name was Paul – then asked, 'Why is there a golden snake lying along the front of your desk pretending to be a ruler?'

It's true, our friend Lanmo was lying very still on the teacher's desk so that he could listen and find out how humans taught their young without the help of educational eggs.

The teacher looked at her desk and, of course, could not see the wonderful snake, because wonderful snakes are not permitted on desks and do not form any part of National Tests and are therefore invisible. She was, however, puzzled and quiet for a moment and had a chilly feeling in the pit of her stomach.

While the teacher felt uneasy, the snake raised his slender and perfect head and looked directly at Paul.

Paul gazed back into those two tiny eyes, red as bravery and sunsets, and deep as chasms. The boy felt his heart beating flipperty-pipperty in his chest and understood – because he was an extremely sensible boy – that something remarkable was happening, something educational, something he would have to remember.

And the snake flickered his tongue out and tasted the teacher's bewilderment and the emptiness of the classroom and the dreaming of the children. And he tasted the bright and growing and puzzling brain whirling away inside Paul's head and the light and clean and flipperty-pipperty heart in his chest.

Then the snake winked at Paul.

This made Paul giggle.

And while Paul was giggling, the snake vanished, just as Paul had guessed a wonderful snake might. This made Paul giggle even more.

'Why are you giggling, you silly boy?' shouted the teacher. Whenever she felt unsure or foolish she would cheer herself up by shouting. All the children understood this; it was part of their education.

'I'm not,' said Paul. He wasn't lying, because he had stopped giggling now. He said this with great certainty, because suddenly he felt certain of all kinds of things and a little bit taller. And somehow his certainty made the teacher recall that she had to make sure the class copied down the National Answers to the National Questions exactly as they should and so she left him be and did some more shouting.

Once she was distracted, Paul grinned a big grin, one he could feel right down in his toes.

When it was time for the lunch break all the children went out into the playground and played various games. Over by the fence Paul surprised himself by scoring a goal in his football game. And near the outside of the Measuring Department two little girls with Very Attractive curly blonde hair were skipping with their Very Attractive Friends.

Lanmo was perched on Mary's shoulder, curled up small like a brooch with only one of his ruby eyes showing. He wanted to learn about playing and what children were like when they were away from teachers and out in the wild. 'Mary, your school is a very strange place.'

Mary whispered to him out of the side of her mouth, 'I think it's quite a normal kind of school, really.'

Lanmo thought for a moment. 'That explains a great deal.'

Mary was in a happy mood because she had a friend and, although usually she wouldn't have tried any such thing, she walked up to the tallest of the Very Attractive Girls gathered beside the Measuring Department and asked, 'May I play at skipping with you?' She was a polite girl.

'*Fffuh*,' said the Very Attractive Girl. We won't bother with her name. She isn't nice.

Mary didn't know what '*fffuh*' meant, so she asked again, 'May I, please?' And waited quietly.

'No, of course you can't. You're weird and you smell of vegetables and your dress is old-old-old, and we all saw you whispering to your shoulder like a mad witch.'

At this, every one of the other Very Attractive Girls began to dance and hop prettily round Mary and to chant, 'Mad witch, mad witch, Mary, Mary, mad witch. Mad witch, mad witch, Mary, Mary, mad witch.'

Naturally, this kind of thing always made Mary feel horrible and if she hadn't tried very hard not to she would have burst into tears. Today she was with her friend Lanmo and so she just stood very still and folded her arms and looked at her scuffed old shoes that were a bit too small. She was sad and her shoes made her even sadder.

But on her shoulder, Lanmo was bristling his scales with fury. This sounded like someone dragging a sword along stones in the far, far distance. He was so furious that he actually began to rattle and he wasn't that kind of snake at all. He lifted his head and said in his most persuasive voice, loudly and clearly, 'You should start skipping again, girls who are not beautiful. That's what you would like to do right now.'

Although the Very Attractive Girls weren't exactly sure who had suggested this, they stopped dancing and chanting and did indeed organise themselves into a line waiting to skip while a pair of girls held the ends of a big skipping rope.

Except, of course, they were not holding the ends of a big skipping rope, because the snake had rushed down from Mary's shoulder and grown into an extremely long and flexible shape and he had made sure that he appeared to be a much more persuasive rope than the real rope. Because sometimes magnificent lies are much easier to believe than boring truths, the girls had duly picked him up and now began to swing him back and forth and round and round and to leap across him. He found this rather delightful and, as Mary watched, he glittered and glistened in the winter sunlight and flickered his tongue while he gathered up news of how mean and tiny the Very Attractive Girls were inside.

This made Mary laugh and clap her hands together.

Now, skipping over a snake is a strange game and has special rules. It makes odd things happen. Without in any way meaning to, the Very Attractive Girls found that they were skipping faster and faster and faster. Their tiny, shapely feet were kicking and stepping in ways that they never had and the arms of the Very Attractive Girls who were turning what they thought was a rope were impossible to see clearly any more, because their arms were swirling round so high and low and terribly quickly. The snake shone and chuckled as the Very Attractive Girls' arms and legs and bodies jumped and flapped and twirled and windmilled, and they all grew hot and tired and worried. But then the Very Attractive Girls became scared.

Mary saw their Very Attractive Faces change, and although it pleased her a tiny bit that they were unhappy, she also felt sorry for them. 'Lanmo, perhaps you should stop now.'

But the snake was having too much fun. He was also still furious.

Slowly, everyone in the playground stopped what they were doing and stared in amazement at the huge, strange, glittering, blurring shape which the pelting girls and the lashing snake now made. Even Paul stopped running around with his jumper pulled over his head because he had scored yet another goal — which made three.

'Lanmo, please,' Mary said, extra quietly.

And because Mary had said please and meant it and because she was his friend, Lanmo did stop, extremely suddenly, by changing his shape again and sliding out of the Very Attractive Girls' sore and weary hands. At this, the girls mostly fell over, or stumbled about as if they must be dizzy. One of them was sick. And, to be honest, they no longer looked even a Tiny Bit Attractive. Their perfectly formed faces were red and sweaty, their carefully-prepared-this-morning hair was knotted and tangled and their willowy limbs were jangled and twitchy. Not one of the Very Attractive Girls mentioned this, but they knew it in their hearts, and when they looked at each other they were dismayed.

Meanwhile, Lanmo wasn't finished. He altered himself again to become the shape of a golden cobra. Cobras, as you will know, have a broad hood that they spread to either side of their head and neck. They also enjoy rearing up impressively and perhaps hissing, and some can even spit venom if they are annoyed. Lanmo was still extremely annoyed, you'll remember, and so he had decided to become a magnificent cobra as tall as a tall grown-up. For a few moments this meant that everyone in the playground couldn't avoid seeing him very clearly for what he was. Even the headmaster, glancing out of his office window, was unable to stop himself noticing that there was a giant glimmering golden cobra rising from the dirty tarmac of the playground. The sight of it made him want to lie down at once until everything went back to normal, and so he hid under his desk. Once he was there, he shut his eyes and pretended that nothing was wrong so hard that he was never quite the same again.

Down in the playground, Lanmo was ignoring the children who were now running up and down and screaming and waving their arms about in highly satisfying ways. He was peering into the eyes of the Very Attractive Girl who had been so rude to Mary. As a result of this, the Very Attractive Girl couldn't move. She could only stare back.

And Lanmo gently, gently opened his mouth and let the world see his needle teeth that were as white as bones.

'No,' said Mary. 'Please, Lanmo.' And she reached out her hand to stop the snake from perhaps doing something wicked.

Lanmo was so furious that he didn't quite notice Mary in time to stop himself as he darted his head forwards and so his smallest, smallest tooth just brushed the edge of her right hand.

And so then Mary fell.

Mary woke up at home in her own little bed. She felt tired, but also really hungry and excited. It was dark, so a number of hours must have passed since she was in the playground. Over to her left, when she looked about, she could see the glow of Lanmo's eyes. He was no longer in the form of a vast and terrifying cobra. He was perhaps a bit smaller than usual and he seemed thinner. He wriggled gently towards her and rubbed his warm forehead against her ear. Then he said to her in his best and kindest voice, 'I am so sorry. I was angry.'

'What happened? Did I faint?'

'That is what the grown-ups have decided to think. They have told everyone that cobras never come to this country and are never golden or as tall as a tall grown-up when they stand. They have decided that

37

nothing especially unusual happened today, or could ever happen, and that everyone must have been asleep and dreaming the same dream. The school will now give pupils new tests on standing up, falling over and sleeping. There will also be Dream Examination Forms to take home and fill in so that all possibly dangerous dreams can be recorded and monitored. And the head-master has retired to take up beekeeping.'

Mary nodded. 'Yes, I suppose all that would happen. Those are the kinds of things they would do.' Children are good at understanding grown-ups, but grown-ups are rarely able to understand children, which is odd because they have already been children and ought to remember what it's like.

Lanmo whispered, 'Your mother and father were worried about you. They borrowed the school janitor's wheelbarrow and brought you home in it and then they put you to bed. They have only just left you, because I pushed the idea into their heads that you are all better now and they can leave you be and go to sleep.'

'Am I better?'

The snake rubbed her ear again. 'My bite is a serious bite. I am so sorry. Even brushing my littlest tooth with your hand was enough to take the colour from twenty-one of your lovely hairs. When you look tomorrow you will see that you have a white streak now, going back from your forehead.' He paused. 'It will be something to talk about when you are older and will seem dramatic.' He paused again. 'I truly am very sorry. Your white hairs show that I have taken a tiny piece of your livingness from you.'

But Mary was very young and full of livingness so this did not worry her. 'Am I better now, though?'

'You are as better as humans get.'

'Will you stay with me? I like you. Only maybe you shouldn't go to school with me again. In case anyone else is nasty to me and makes you cross.'

'I think you will find that no one is nasty to you at school, not ever again. They will be very polite to you from now on,' said the snake, sounding as boastful as he usually did. Only then he whispered more gloomily, 'I will stay until the morning, but then I will go away for a while.'

This worried Mary much more than having twenty-one white hairs. 'Why?'

'I am going because I feel guilty and I have never felt guilty before. I harmed you. I have to think about this until I understand it.'

'Well, how long will it take you to think? And where will you think and will it be nice and will you be able to get cheese there?' asked Mary, because the snake was her friend.

'I will be safe. I am never in danger,' said Lanmo, making all of those words seem a bit sad.

'You didn't mean to hurt me. And I don't really mind.' Mary imagined her white streak and how it would be an exciting thing and pictured herself being a remarkable woman in exploring clothes and adventuring boots with her dramatic hair blowing about in the wind on the top of a mountain she had just climbed.

Lanmo sighed, tasting her thoughts with his clever tongue. 'Yes, being an explorer with a white streak in your hair would be exciting. You may say that you were changed by an encounter with an extraordinary and beautiful snake if you like.'

'Oh, no,' replied Mary. 'I will say it was caused by a shark bite.'

'As you wish. Although some of my finest acquaintances are sharks. Sleep now, though, because you should rest.'

'But I don't wa—' began Mary, because she would rather have talked all night to Lanmo and persuaded him not to go away. But *he* had persuaded *her* with his eyes that she should sleep. He was *extremely* persuasive.

When it was dawn and Mary woke, Lanmo was snuggled under her chin, all warm like a little scarf.

She felt him wriggle as if he were pretending to be cheerful and not quite managing. Then he slipped along to rest on her pillow and look at her. 'You may kiss my nose if you wish.'

Mary did so, frowning a little because this seemed like goodbye.

'You must now take care of yourself for a while. Try to ignore your teachers without offending them. And do not talk to any other snakes. And avoid lions. And sharks. You will find that the girls like you now, although you will discover most of them are boring to speak with and quite unpleasant. Their eggs must have had nothing at all written inside them. You might enjoy talking to the ginger-headed boy called Paul. And when you eat cheese you can think of me . . . And when the sun sets I will wish you sweet dreams and you will have them. That is how you will know I am thinking of you and that you are my friend and I am yours.'

'Well, when will you come back?'

'When I have learned not to be angry.'

'Do you still feel guilty?'

'Yes.'

'Why should you be guilty when I have forgiven you and I would like you to stay?'

'I don't know, but I think that is how being guilty

works. I will return as soon as I can.' And then the snake shimmered all his scales so that he looked especially beautiful to remember and he flickered his tongue at her ear and he sighed. After that he was gone.

The snake Mary called Lanmo was away from her for a month and then another month and then for much longer than Mary would have liked. She kept a tally of the days in her notebook so that she could be cross with him when he did appear. Then she kept a tally so that she could show him she had missed him very much and noticed that he hadn't been with her.

In the meantime, she went to school and found the other pupils were, indeed, as nice to her as they could manage. Most of them were quite boring. She learned her lessons quietly, even though she didn't always agree with them, and sometimes she went for walks with the boy called Paul and they would collect bottle tops, or string, or discuss new names for stars and what the moon might be thinking and whether it minded very much when it shrank to a curvy line, or swelled up to a silver-yellow eye that stared.

Whatever she did, she never forgot the snake, and when she rested her head on her pillow she wished Lanmo well and then enjoyed the wonderful dreams he sent her. She never mentioned those dreams on her Dream Assessment Form, of course; she just made things up about riding ponies and making pies.

A way from Mary, the snake she called Lanmo travelled to many far lands in the world and many near lands. He rode in tiny boats and wriggled into deep mines full of gold and coal and all manner of other substances which humans believe to be precious. He looked out across desert cities from the tops of new buildings in construction and looked out across rubble and dust from the ruins of buildings which had been destroyed. He sat up nicely in expensive restaurants and lay under pillows in hospitals. He slipped very delicately here and there in great towns built out of tents and slid along inside little wooden shelters and into shallow wells and cups and between folded blankets. He watched at the corners of streets next to busy crossings and quiet crossings and lounged across the dashboards of cars. He was very busy. Lanmo was always very busy. He could not remember a time when he had been idle, although he did, if he thought about it hard, recall a time when there had been far fewer humans and more trees. Lanmo liked trees. They were good for climbing. Sometimes he sent Mary special dreams where the two of them journeyed through old, old forests and scrambled and undulated together up to the highest branches where they could see the sunrise and be immensely glad together. This made him happy. It was much better than just climbing up and then climbing back down again.

The snake knew that he would have been much busier had it not been for humans helping him with his work. When night rolled over the curve of the world and across whichever country he was visiting, Lanmo would sometimes be able to rest and curl himself into a coil and flicker his clever tongue through the breeze so that he could taste how many, many times the humans of each darkened land were busy instead of him. They worked hard and saved him the task of visiting this or that other human and showing them his needle teeth as white as bones and making them hear his beautiful voice and look into his honest red eyes. But this did not make Lanmo love the humans. In fact it made him think rather badly of them, although his opinion made no difference to either the humans or his duties.

One evening, Lanmo came to call upon a grand-mother. Lanmo met a lot of grandmothers. This granny was seventy-seven years, three months and fourteen days old and she was called Mrs Dorothy Higginbottom. When the snake arrived at the foot of Granny Higginbottom's bed she was sitting up in it, leaning against her pillows and turning over a page in her magazine about terrible things happening to strangers and amusing things happening to cats. Unlike many of the other grandmothers, as Granny Higginbottom glanced beyond a picture of a cat wearing a knitted waistcoat and looking annoyed, she was able to see Lanmo.

She put down her magazine. 'Hello,' she said in a whispery grandmothery voice.

'Hello,' said Lanmo in his best pearls-and-chocolate voice. 'I have come—'

'Oh, I know,' interrupted Granny Higginbottom. 'I know quite well why you have come and I am content, but I would like to talk a while, if you don't mind.'

Since leaving Mary, because he had been too angry and then too guilty, Lanmo had missed talking to a sensible human. This meant he was happy to smooth along, all the way up the bed, until he could rest on the covers above Granny Higginbottom's lap. 'What would you like to talk about?'

'Well, I suppose it is too late to discuss most things.'

The snake nodded and made himself comfortable in the warmth of the quilt. He waited. Although he was always busy, he was never in a hurry. That was the nature of the snake.

Granny Higginbottom began: 'I think I would like to tell someone how much I dislike my grandchildren. They are very mean-spirited and when they come to visit they bring me grapefruit which I do not like and presents that other people have given them and which they don't want. I once found a little card they had forgotten to remove from one offering – a plastic box

49

containing nail clippers and a nose-hair remover. The card said: "Please enjoy this free gift from *Gentleman's Grooming Monthly*."'

'That is unimpressive,' said the snake. No one but Mary had ever given him any kind of present. She had given him food and kisses and conversation and company.

'Quite,' said Granny Higginbottom. 'I gave birth to three children – two girls and a boy. I loved them and showed them sunsets and the insides of apples and let them hear the voices in shells and we walked in meadows and slid on slides, but the boy and one of the girls were only ever interested in shiny pennies and gossip and making their other sister cry. And the children they gave birth to and raised are terrible children. My cruel daughter and my cruel son come and visit me with their herds of ghastly offspring every Sunday. While some of them stay in here with me, I can hear the rest of them searching my house for nice ornaments to sell, or jewels, or money. I ask them, "What is that noise of someone lifting up my floorboards?" and they tell me, "Nothing, silly Granny – it's the wind in the rafters." I ask them, "What's that noise like greedy fingers opening my boxes and rifling through my cupboards?" and they tell me, "It's just the rats in this big, old house, silly Granny. You should let us sell it and move you into a home." And I ask them, "What's that sound like my pictures being taken down and my chairs being carried away?" and they tell me, "You are going mad in your old age, silly Granny, and you should let us put you in a home at once and take care of all your belongings so they don't bother you any longer." It has begun to wear me out. The only pleasant thing they do is send me a bunch of roses on the first day of January. Roses are my favourite and they make my new year smell sweet and they fill it with colours.'

'That would be pleasant,' agreed the snake, tasting the essence of Granny Higginbottom which was kind and puzzled and very, very tired. 'What happened to your other daughter?'

'I don't know. I think they sent her away. Or maybe they drove her away. Inside my mattress I have hidden my engagement ring and my wedding ring and the ring my husband gave me when we had been married for forty years — that was just before he died — and I have also tucked away four jewels and sixteen gold pieces. That is all I have worth having and it is for my good daughter, but I do not know where to send it. When I am gone my dreadful other daughter and my horrible son and their ghastly children will come and take everything.' Granny Higginbottom fell silent and looked very sad. Since the snake had left Mary he understood a lot more about being sad.

The snake tasted the air again with his wise, quick tongue. 'Your daughter is in the land which is four lands to the left of here and two lands higher.'

'And is she safe?'

The snake's tongue flickered again, fast as fast can be. He thought for a moment. 'She is safe and comfortable and content. There is only one part of her that is sad and that is the part which remembers you. Your other children told her they would harm you if she didn't go away and never write and never try to send you any messages. But on the first day of January every year she has sent you roses to make your new year sweet and fill it with colours.'

'Ah.' Granny Higginbottom's eyes became a deeper blue and she shed tears which tasted to Lanmo of the moon and other wildernesses. Then she smiled. 'That explains it.' She patted the quilt near Lanmo's head. 'Is it time for us to begin?'

'Well . . . usually . . . yes.' But Lanmo paused and thought; the old lady had lived so long she might know many things. So he asked her, 'I have lately been very angry. And I have also felt guilt for the first time.

This troubles me. And I have wandered the earth, and the anger and the guilt have not left me. They have been as close as my shadow.'

'Hmmm . . .' Granny Higginbottom tickled behind his ear, which he normally wouldn't have allowed, but it seemed to comfort him. 'Then you love someone. How strange. I didn't think you would.'

'Love?'

'To be very angry, you must first have loved very much, or have been very much afraid. Now, I do not think you could be afraid of anything or anyone . . .'

'That is true,' Lanmo nodded. 'At least, I think that is true.'

When Granny Higginbottom heard doubt in Lanmo's voice she added, 'Not unless perhaps you were afraid for that which you love . . . Is there something you love, snake?'

'No.'

'Ah. Then there is some*one* you love.'

At this, Lanmo found he could not manage to say anything in his wonderful voice. He simply leaned against the old lady's hand and let her gently rub his golden scales in a way that he liked and that reminded him of his friend Mary. Granny Higginbottom told him quietly, 'Love is a terrible thing.'

'So it seems,' whispered Lanmo.

'But it is also wonderful.'

'Perhaps.' He eased a little nearer Granny Higginbottom. 'Perhaps it is.' Then he looked into her eyes with great seriousness. 'I promise that I will take your three rings and your four jewels and your sixteen gold pieces away with me before anyone else can find them. I will carry them to your daughter's house. She will recognise your rings and she will know you sent them.'

'And will you meet with her?' Granny Higginbottom sounded worried.

'No. I will not meet with your daughter for a long while yet,' said Lanmo. 'But I swear that I will give her your treasures.'

'I would not have thought you were the kind of snake to make promises.'

'I am not.' The snake came as close to smiling as he could. 'But maybe I am changing,' he explained. 'I am not sure.'

The old lady smiled and laid her head back against her pillows and closed her eyes. Then she let Lanmo, who had made himself very small, tuck in under her chin.

'Good night, snake, and thank you.'

'I need not be thanked,' whispered the snake.

'Will this be quick?'

'This will be quick and this will be for ever,' said the snake. 'Good night, Granny Higginbottom.'

And when he was done the snake took up the old lady's treasures and wriggled them onto his back which he made very broad and safe, like a golden dish, and he rushed over the lands between him and the lost daughter's house. When he reached her threshold he tested the air one last time and was sure that the daughter had a heart as good and deep as her mother had once had until it fell still. Then Lanmo whisked, faster than anyone could have seen, in under doors and behind furniture and he left the three rings, the four jewels and the sixteen gold pieces on the kitchen table.

In the morning, Granny Higginbottom's lost daughter came downstairs to discover her twin girls playing with bright gold pieces and jewels and with three rings that she recognised at once as belonging to her mother.

The daughter sat down then and cried although her children did not know why, and she hugged them very close. And when her husband came downstairs, ready for his breakfast, she held him, too, and she called out a loud and red and towering word from no language that any of them spoke and yet they understood it. They clung to each other and the snake tasted that they were sad and also that they were covered in love.

The snake watched them from a shadow between the saucepans and then he went away and was busy in the many different countries that humans had marked out across the earth to keep themselves divided.

While Lanmo carried out his duties among the peoples of the world, Mary performed her duties as a little girl. She grew older and taller and her arms and legs were sometimes exceptionally clumsy and sometimes exceptionally graceful – she just didn't know which would happen when and that was rather tiresome for her. Mary performed her duties as a schoolgirl, too, and learned the National Limits of Happiness and the Leisure Percentages and the names of prominent generals, living and dead, and the movements of troops during various famous campaigns. She taught herself how to spell marvellously long and interesting words like *photolithography* and also tasty words like *peristalsis* and *reticulatus*. And she also taught herself how to hop on the spot without stopping (she could get up to nearly three hundred and fifty) and how to burn toast. She had learned all of her mother's smiles and all of her father's hugs and vice versa. She was quite happy. When she had spare moments, she would play in the tiny garden and daydream about exploring. When it was cold, she would imagine standing on the back of a sledge and asking her huskies to pull her — *padpadpadpadpadpadpad* — across snowfields and past polar bears and penguins who would admire her caribou-skin parka and her look of determination. When it was hot, she imagined walking in desert mountains the colour of biscuits in sturdy boots and talking to lizards, or squeezing through the gaps in jungles.

'You must never squeeze through gaps in jungles.' Mary looked down and there was the neat shape of Lanmo around her wrist, blinking at her, maybe a little nervously. The snake angled his head as if he would like to nuzzle her palm, but didn't know if she would like it. 'You are longer than I remember. And your hair has swelled. You are very changeable.'

Mary was delighted to see her friend, but also annoyed because more than two years had passed since the snake had last appeared and she felt it was inconsiderate of him to be away for such a large amount of time. 'And you are very late. You haven't been to visit me for eight hundred and twelve days, three hours and several minutes. I have written out the days in my notebook, if you would like to check.'

'I'm sorry.' Lanmo did look sorry. 'I lost track of the time.'

'That's no excuse,' Mary said.

'And I had a great deal to do.'

The snake was mumbling because he felt ashamed, but even so Mary couldn't help enjoying his beautiful voice and being glad that he was there. She decided to sound cross a little longer, though, to teach him a lesson. 'Now you sound like a grown-up. They are always being busy instead of doing the things that are important.'

'Promise me with all your heart and your entire attention that you will not ever squeeze through gaps in the jungle – they might contain poisonous spiders, or sharp thorns, or impolite and unpleasant and shockingly ugly snakes. And be careful in deserts because the sands also contain spiders and rude and horrifying snakes and scorpions and mountain lions. Be careful everywhere. In fact, perhaps you should stay in your city instead.'

Mary lifted her hand so that the snake was level with her face and smiled at her friend and kissed his head with great solemnity. 'Welcome back, Lanmo. I would offer you some cheese, but we have none. There has been a difficulty with the railway lines that go to the countryside where they keep the cows and the milk.' She spun round and round after that, because she was so full of happiness, and she laughed in a way that Lanmo was sure no other human could laugh. He shivered his scales so that they made a silvery noise, like someone with cool fingers playing a crystal harp far away in a peaceful place. He found that he was as happy as his friend.

Still, as he and Mary spun round, he noticed that the city looked a good deal sadder than he remembered. There were angry words painted on some of the walls and the pavements were broken in places and not clean. There were fewer kites flying and the ones that did fly looked as if they had simply been forgotten and left alone on the rooftops and balconies with no one caring. He licked the air and it no longer tasted of laughter. In the direction of the shining towers there were even more high buildings with even more sharp edges cutting at the sky. The new towers tasted empty.

And in the little garden, Mary's parents had planted beans and cabbages around the roses. They had also added pots containing herbs and tomatoes and a deep tub which was trying to hold potato plants. The plants looked quite angry and as if they didn't want to make potatoes this year, or maybe ever.

'Oh, but let me show you this,' said Mary and ran into her house, carrying the snake balanced on her palm like a tiny emperor with no arms and legs. 'There,' she announced, coming to a halt. (There was never far to run in Mary's apartment.) In the corner of the tiny kitchen, playing with a little wooden ball, was a kitten that Mary's parents had allowed her to have. The kind lady who owned the bakery had a mother cat who had given birth to four kittens: a white and orange and brown one, a white and grey and brown one, a ginger and white one and a black-all-over one. The black-all-over one had the cleverest eyes and so Mary had picked it.

The bakery lady needed cats to stop the mice and rats from eating the flour. There were a lot of rats now, but she couldn't afford to feed more than two cats to chase them, so she had to give away all but two of the kittens. She could also no longer afford to give away bread.

The snake studied the kitten for a moment, 'Wonderful,' he said and then, before Mary could say anything at all, Lanmo had sleeked down from her hand and onto the floor, opening his mouth wider and wider as he went. He then began to swallow the kitten, beginning with its head and its front paws.

'No!' cried Mary.

At this, the snake frowned and stopped moving. The kitten's back legs wriggled as they poked out of Lanmo's mouth and Mary could hear a quizzical *meooommh?* from inside the snake as the kitten tried to ask what was happening, because it had never been swallowed by anything before.

'*Gnnnph?*' asked the snake in return.

'No, no, no,' said Mary. 'That is Shade and he is my kitten and you are not to eat him, not even a bit.'

'*Gmmngn?*'

'You are not to eat my kitten.'

The snake sighed as well as a snake can with its mouth full of kitten. '*Gngngn-agh-agh-kkkahh,*' he said as he gradually coughed up the kitten. The snake then wriggled his head and shook, until the kitten dropped out of his mouth and ended up sitting – looking rather surprised and wet – on the kitchen floor. The kitten blinked and then sneezed – *meooff* – and started to lick its fur back into the proper order.

Lanmo used his most formal and embarrassed voice, standing up so that he looked very slightly like a short, respectable gentleman made of gold with some of the bits missing. 'I am sorry, Mary. I misunderstood. I thought because you had no cheese that you were giving me this delicious . . . I mean this lovely kitten to . . . um . . .' He said this last word very softly, 'Eat.'

'I was introducing you.'

'Mary, you should never introduce kittens to snakes.'

'But you're not a snake – you're my friend.'

Lanmo slid carefully away from the kitten, who was now lying on his back and playing with his own paws, just as if he hadn't nearly been dinner only a few moments before. 'I am your friend.' He cleared his throat. 'But I am also a snake. And a snake is a snake is a snake.' He flickered out his tongue to taste if he was forgiven and then he darted forwards like poured metal and reappeared on Mary's hand and reached up to tickle her eyebrows with his tongue. 'I think it made me sad not to see you.'

'Well, I know it made me sad not to see you.'

After this, Mary explained that she had an appointment and that she wished she had known the snake was coming, but that it was Saturday and Saturday was a day for appointments.

'May I come with you?'

'I don't think so,' Mary told him and then she went away to her little room and came back smelling of lilies and wearing an extremely pleasant dress which she had bought from a neighbour and altered herself, because she did, after all, know how to sew quite well, even though learning how had been irritating.

The snake did not wish to pry and so did not taste the air around her, but let her go. Then Lanmo pretended to be string all afternoon so that the kitten could play with him. At first this was slightly humiliating, but eventually the snake rather liked wriggling just the end of his tail and then dashing away when the kitten pounced, or rubbing the kitten's tummy and making him purr, or darting underneath him, so that he fell over into a soft heap. Once the kitten was tired – and it takes a long time to tire out a kitten – the snake wound itself into coils like a basket and the kitten slept inside his warm scales with one soft paw lolling over the side. When Mary's parents came home after spending the day at a market, selling a few ornaments and pictures they did not need, they simply saw the dozing kitten and assumed that it must be asleep on a blanket or in a basket, because kittens are never known to sleep in the arms of snakes. (Of course snakes don't have arms, but they can hug people and animals if they choose to.)

When Mary came back home, she seemed especially happy and was singing a little song under her breath.

You are the night with sunshine
You are the ocean with no shore
You are the bird that sings wine
You are the lion with no claw.
And be my honour and be mine
And be my glory and be mine
And be my living and be mine
My friend, my love, be mine.

During dinner, the snake waited patiently under Mary's napkin while she and her parents ate their bread made of apologetic flour with specks of sand in it and drank their soup made of cabbage leaves from the garden and water and a handful of rice.

Then the little family sat together on the couch – which was most of their furniture – all snuggled and huddled under a big rug against the cold. Mary was tucked in between her parents and Lanmo was tucked in with her, his clever head and his observant eyes peeping over the top of the blanket. He liked being warm like this and feeling what a human home was like. The snake couldn't help noticing, though, that the bright rug that used to cover the shabby floorboards of the living-room had disappeared and so had the vase that used to stand on the table with its wide mouth open, asking for flowers. And the table had gone, too.

Mary's father read to everyone by the yellowy glow of a tired lightbulb. He chose a story they all enjoyed and knew almost by heart about a lucky young woodcutter's son who once gave a cup of water to a thirsty old lady who passed by his garden. The old lady appeared to be poor and scraggly and perhaps a little bit strange, but it turned out that she was a magical person and kept on granting the woodcutter wishes and making him have adventures and introducing him to knights in armour and wizards. The woodcutter found all this a bit alarming and wasn't always pleased to wake up in a crystal mountain with a task to carry out, or to be sent off on a quest to find something impossible, but he was polite and just carried on anyway. In the end, while he was voyaging between peculiar islands in a talking boat, he met a very kind and lovely stonemason who ended up being his wife, so mostly he was glad that he had given the old lady a drink when she needed it.

Mary's father decided to read out the passage where the woman on the island puts down her chisel and confesses her undying love. While he did this, Mary's mother nudged her once or twice, and it was clear to the snake that both Mary's parents were trying to suggest that she might herself have found someone she liked as much as a stonemason might love a woodcutter. Mary kept rather quiet about all this, but she did giggle now and then and squeeze the snake's tail slightly too hard when a sentence involving a first kiss was recited.

When the electricity was turned off at nine p.m., because of the rationing, everyone said goodnight and kissed and wished everyone sweet dreams and then got ready to sleep. Mother used the bathroom first and then Father and then Mary.

Once she had turned out her light and slipped into bed, Lanmo settled on her pillow in a contented coil as he had wanted to for so long, his eyes glowing gently. He asked her, 'Mary, can you tell me about love?'

'I don't know what you mean,' said Mary and blushed so that the snake could feel it in the darkness. This was perhaps the only lie she ever told the snake, although probably we can forgive her, because very few humans understand all there is to know about love and maybe she didn't want to say something wrong and mislead her friend.

'Mary, for many, many centuries I have travelled in every land of the earth and I have met many, many humans. At one time I did my work amongst them without troubling myself to know or understand them. This was partly because they seem very complicated and strange creatures and partly because they do not last very long. Since I met you I have paid them more attention and I have been able to recognise the taste of love in a great number of them. Some of them love places and some of them love things and some of them love themselves and some of them love other people. You taste of the love of other people.'

'Well, I love you. You are my friend. And you are here.'

The snake tasted the air and coughed in a way that indicated he was a little bit impatient and would like Mary to be plain with him. 'That has a nice taste,' he said. 'It tastes of fresh mice and the steam from ironing clean clothes and of sunshine.' He looked at her very deeply with his intelligent red eyes. 'But you also taste of the love which is for one particular person whom you want to kiss a great deal. That taste is flavoured with honeysuckle and pepper.'

'Oh . . .' Mary hugged herself and smiled in a way that made the room brighter. 'That boy you said I should talk to who was called Paul . . . He and I like bats and cats and we enjoy floating and boating and we listen to the stars together while we lie on the riverbank where the grass is soft and . . .'

'Yes?' said the snake, feeling a bit jealous.

'He is a wonderful person. Not wonderful because he is magic like you, but wonderful because he is Paul.'

'Am I not wonderful because I am Lanmo?'

'Of course you are,' said Mary, but then she rushed on to a long description of Paul's hair and how he walked and the funny and clever things he said, and although Lanmo tried very hard to be glad for her because she was so full-up-to-the-top with joy, he did also get quite bored. Eventually, he fell asleep.

I t was almost time for the sun to rise when Lanmo woke. In fact, he had been woken by Mary's voice finally trailing off into silence. This was not because she had run out of good things to say about Paul, it was simply because she had eventually become too tired to be quite so heartily in love and so her body had insisted that she drift away into a dream about exploring fascinating caves full of jewels and seams of silver and gold and stalactites lollopping down from the vaulted roofs and stalagmites lollopping upwards. Paul was not with her in her dream and this was the beginning of her realising that loving him might mean she would not become a famous adventurer after all. Not unless he also liked adventures. Somehow, she had never managed to mention her plans for being an explorer to Paul. This was because they were very important to her and she didn't want Paul to laugh at them, or snort down his nose the way he snorted down his nose when they talked about the silly people who couldn't hear the stars and the silly people who liked lying on carpets and sofas when they could lie on the soft grass instead and feel it tickle and inhale its scent.

While Mary dreamed, the snake sleeked as fast as love to the home of a Great Man Who Loved the People. It was perched on the edge of a cliff with long, high windows that looked out over the ocean and got a perfect view of the storms and the sunsets and passing pods of whales and dolphins. The Great Man Who Loved the People would sometimes open his windows and walk out onto his balcony and stand with his nose pointed into the flattering breeze, wearing his very plain suit that showed he was humble and his very ordinary shoes that showed he was trust-worthy and his mildly patterned tie that showed he was sensitive and artistic but not too wild. He felt it was only fair to allow the ocean to look up at a man as wonderful as he was and to be glad as a result. He was sure the whales and dolphins would also find their lives improved by knowing he was there. And now and then he would declaim phrases across the waves to see if they sounded sufficiently inspiring and magnificent. All this was done on behalf of the people, of course, because he was always very humble and mindful of the people.

On this early, early morning, the Great Man Who Loved the People had been unable to sleep. Yesterday he had received a communication from one of his generals telling him that the war he was conducting on behalf of the people had killed eighty per cent of the enemies of the people. There was only one enemy city left standing, the City of Thoth. It was filled with women and children and the elderly. The general had written to say that the City of Thoth had surrendered and that the war could be over soon, which was good because seventy-five per cent of the Great Man Who Loved the People's people had died fighting it. Everyone wanted a rest now. The Great Man Who Loved the People had thought all night about what would be the most merciful and wise thing to do under these circumstances because he had a soft and refined heart and was tender towards the elderly and always kissed women and children in respectful and popular ways as an expression of love for his people. After much consideration, he had called an official messenger and given him a letter for the general.

The letter read:

Dear General and Commander-in-Chief of
Our Magnificent Forces,

As your humble and loving leader I thank you
for your brave service on behalf of the people.
I thank you also for your news of the war. The
City of Thoth, you say, contains the elderly
who are left amongst our enemies. The elderly,
as you will know, remember much and contain
a great deal of wisdom. If the memory and the
wisdom of our enemies remain, then they may
rise again and defeat us. Therefore the elderly
must be killed. The women of our enemies
also remain alive there. They may give birth to
a new generation of enemies and may harbour
feminine resentments about our treatment of
their people. Therefore the women must be
killed. The children left alive in the city may
grow up to be enemies more vengeful than
those we already have and may bear further
children and eventually fill the world with
deadly foes. Therefore the children must be
killed. Twenty-five per cent of my beloved
people still remain alive. They have not nobly
sacrificed themselves in my defence of their
way of life. They have not already wiped the

dangerous and threatening City of Thoth from the face of the earth. This means they must be traitors. Therefore the remainder of my people must be killed. Once your men have carried out these necessary measures for the defence of my people, you must explain to them that because they had not already killed the traitors hidden in our glorious country (and the evil citizens of the City of Thoth) they are traitors. Therefore they must kill each other and then themselves. You, my loyal and brave commander, have asked me to end the Great War on Behalf of the People. This means you are not true to the wonderful aims of our Great War on Behalf of the People. You are a traitor. Therefore, once you are sure that everyone else is dead, you must kill yourself.

I send this message with all brotherly love and fellowship, my very dear General.

The Great Man Who Loved the People read this message aloud a few times to make sure it was sufficiently filled with love and justice. Then he reached out to place the letter in the shaking hands of the now pale-faced messenger.

Perhaps to delay his departure for what would be certain death, the messenger asked, 'Why, oh Glorious Leader, is there a golden snake wound around the railing of your balcony?'

The Great Man Who Loved the People laughed at such a suggestion, but he did turn to study the railing and, strangely, did notice that a beautiful snake he had never seen before was resting there. The snake was twitching the end of his tail and watching him with deeply red eyes. Those eyes disturbed the Great Man Who Loved the People. (We will call him GMWLtP from now on, because his name is too long and he won't be needing it soon.) They reminded him of the light from the first city he had burned, many years before.

'Good morning,' said the snake.

This made the GMWLtP drop his letter and not even notice the messenger running from the balcony. The messenger kept running from the ballroom beyond it and down the stairs and across the courtyard with its lush and extravagant gardens and on and on across battlefields and ruined villages and through burned orchards until he was back in his family's village. Two of his cousins and his mother were still alive there and he stayed with them and never, ever talked about his time with the GMWLtP.

While all that began to happen, the GMWLtP simply stood on the spot and swallowed.

'Over the years you have saved me a great deal of busyness,' said the snake, in his most charming voice. 'You have been determined to do my work for me.' His words fell delicately through the air like silk. 'I do not find that I can like you.' The snake flickered his tongue into the air and tasted the GMWLtP's bewilderment. 'In the past I generally formed no personal opinions about the people I met while I did what I must do. Lately, however, I have been taught to take more interest in the lives of humans and I . . .' He paused for a moment and frowned, although it was difficult to see this because he had no eyebrows and not really any forehead. 'I truly do not like you. Today I am very happy that we have met.'

'But I am the Great Man Who Loves the People,' blustered the GMWLtP.

'No.' The snake blinked and then let his stare sink and burrow and peer all the way into the soul and heart and thinking of the GMWLtP. 'No, you are just Nigel Simon Beech. And I shall enjoy this.'

And the snake opened his mouth and let his teeth shine in the dawn light, as white as bones. Just for a moment.

When Mary awoke, Lanmo was back on her pillow, looking very contentedly at her. There was no sign on even the tiniest of the snake's scales that he had travelled thousands of miles since she last faced him.

'Hello, Mary. Shall we go to school?'

'No, silly – today is a Sunday. So first I will go to the cornershop and sweep up and help to stack the shelves – which is my job. Then after lunch we can walk along the Grand Avenue and eat ice cream. I'm allowed to eat one ice cream paid for out of my wages. My parents need the rest of the money since things have become so difficult in so many ways. And sometimes I get to take home dented tins or broken packets.'

'I don't think I would be very interested in sweeping

and stacking,' said the snake. 'I will stay here with your mother and father until you are done.'

'It is a bit boring sweeping,' agreed Mary. 'And since rationing there isn't very much to stack any more. I mostly just move the tins around. We really need the money I earn, but I think in a few weeks Mr Paphos will say he can't pay me any more.'

Mary looked so sad while she said this that Lanmo felt himself chill all along his spine. Although this taught him a little more about love, it also made him become sad himself and he had the idea that his head hurt and that his eyes stung. To cheer Mary, he rattled his scales so that they sounded like golden feathers on beautiful birds with good hearts and he danced back and forth across her blanket until he was only a shimmer and a glisten of heat and wonder.

This did indeed allow Mary to forget her troubles. Generally, she tried not to be downhearted and was inclined to be a mostly happy person. And, of course, as the snake could taste, she was in love with Paul, and this lit and warmed a space in her through and through in a manner which kept everything but the cloudiest of thoughts at bay.

So, after a breakfast of porridge made with water and some tea without milk, Mary went off to Mr Paphos's shop. Lanmo stayed in the cramped living-room, resting along the top of a skirting board and pretending to be a length of spectacularly lovely wiring. Mary's mother and father cleaned up after breakfast and then sat in silence on their couch. They didn't notice the snake at all, partly because they were grown-ups and partly because they were both staring straight ahead at something they thought they could see in their future, something which they didn't like. After a while Mary's father held his wife's hand and Mary's mother leaned her head on her husband's shoulder.

'It will be all right,' said her mother.

'In the end. Maybe,' said her father.

Neither of them sounded as if they believed this was true.

The snake found that he wanted to stand up as tall as he could and to become awe-inspiring and to announce, 'You must go at once to the Land of Perditi where I know you can be safe for as long as you live! You must listen and go today, or maybe tomorrow morning, and you must take with you only what you can carry for a long, long time without getting tired! Your city is too sad now. Your kites hardly fly. Can't you see that everything has changed? You must leave behind whatever else you have before sad times make you watch it being taken from you! The sad times will do you harm! You must be safe and keep on being alive because Mary loves you and I do . . . I also . . . I have in my heart this thing which is love for Mary!'

But he knew that Mary's parents would not be able to hear or even see him. They would not want him to be there, and really would not want to understand what he said. Humans very often do not want to leave what they have in one place, or go to another place, not until it is too late for them to keep safe.

So Lanmo winked at the kitten, which was resting on Mary's mother's lap and trying to make her feel warm and comfortable. The kitten jumped down – *pompompompom* – onto its soft, pink little feet and followed the tempting flicker and wriggle of Lanmo's tail. And they played together in the tiny garden until both of them were not thinking of anything at all apart from having fun. Sometimes when there is nothing else to do, or nothing that can be done yet, it is best to be happy with friends and to let this strengthen your spirit.

When Mary arrived back from work she was rather dusty and tired, but she was holding a package of broken spaghetti, which made almost everyone delighted. (Lanmo was not fond of spaghetti because it allowed humans to look as if they were eating tiny snakes.) Father hugged Mary and Mother, and Mother hugged Mary and Father, and secretly all the while Lanmo had looped himself around Mary's throat like a necklace so that he could also share in the so many hugs and so much smiling about a small amount of broken pasta. He found it remarkable that humans could persuade themselves to keep going under almost any circumstances and that they were very willing to be joyful and courageous. It was a shame so many of them were so stupid.

The kitten also got hugs and kisses on his nose and a handful of biscuity cat food from Mr Paphos's shop. (Fewer and fewer people were keeping pets and so he could give away pet food without worrying that he would have less to sell – almost no one was buying any.)

The humans enjoyed a lunch of boiled pasta and a small amount of sage and some tomatoes from the garden. Everyone agreed it was a feast. Then Mary changed into her nicest dress (which she had been allowed to make from one of her mother's nicest dresses) and trotted happily outside and headed for the Grand Avenue with Lanmo perched on her shoulder like a very long and thin golden canary.

The Grand Avenue was not so grand as it had been only a few years ago. Many of the high and wide shop windows were empty or boarded up and the market at the corner of Valdemar Street was quiet. Mary had loved it when it was full of heaped spices in aromatic rainbows and colourful fruits and vegetables carefully stacked. Its silk traders had all but disappeared and the leather workers were only selling a very few sandals and grubby, faded bags. But the ice cream cart was still there and Mr Chanson was still selling cones and tubs and icy treats, although no one liked to ask him how he got the cream. His ices were still delicious: strawberry, cake with flaberry, chocolate with lingonberry, plain chocolate, lemon, gooseberry with elderflower and Marionberry.

Mary joined the queue of townspeople anxious to have a little treat and to act as if Sundays were just as enjoyable as always. Lanmo had never eaten ice cream before and it intrigued him. 'Mary, what flavour should I have?'

Mary didn't answer at once and so he slipped along her shoulder, very close to her ear, and asked, 'Is there something wrong?'

'It's just that . . .' whispered Mary, 'I can only afford the one ice cream. My parents need the rest of the money. It wouldn't be fair to buy two.'

'Hmmm,' said Lanmo and smiled as much as he ever could. 'But I can make the human selling ice cream think that we have paid him. I can make him think that we have bought the whole cartload in every flavour.' He chuckled a velvety chuckle that was so warm it might almost have melted the ice cream.

'No, no, no, Lanmo, that would be terrible. Mr Chanson needs the money to buy his mysterious milk and make us more ice cream. We can't steal from him – he's nice. He gives everyone chocolate sprinkles, or sauce, or extra little dabs of ice cream for free.'

Lanmo shrank slightly and leaned against Mary's neck. 'I do not understand humans. Some of you will steal anything all the time and some of you will steal nothing all the time. Couldn't all of you just steal something some of the time – if you need it?'

'I don't think so.'

'But you are hungry and other people have more food than they can eat.'

'Yes, but that is the way of the world.'

Lanmo thought about this and found that it was an unsatisfactory answer. 'That is an unsatisfactory answer,' he said.

'I know,' said Mary. 'But that is the only answer my parents and my teachers have ever given me to the problems of who has food and who does not.'

By this time, our friends were at the head of the ice cream queue and so the snake simply let Mary choose one cone with one scoop of her own favourite flavour, because he had never experienced any of the flavours on offer and didn't know what to pick. 'How do you catch a lemon?'

'Lemons just hang from their trees and stay very still and you can pick them easily. All the fruits are like that.'

'That is very foolish of them. No wonder everybody eats them.' Lanmo licked the air and tasted the sweet and sticky and rich wonderfulness of the ice cream scents. They almost made his head spin. 'Do you like strawberry?' He could not recall when anything last made his head spin.

'Strawberry is my favourite.'

'Then we must have that.'

Mary duly paid for the single scoop of strawberry ice cream and then ambled along to a little bench set under a broad, friendly tree that had stood in the Grand Avenue for many years and had become a landmark and a meeting place for humans. She held the cornet and Lanmo shrank himself and wound his body around it so that his head was just level with the ice cream. The cool of it made him feel slightly sleepy and yet excited. Mary waited while his tongue flickered and fippered and tickled nearer and nearer to the ice cream and then finally took a tiny, tiny, snake-sized lick. 'Mmmmmm.'

After that the friends took turns licking while they sat and watched people pass.

'Mmmnnnmmmnnn,' Lanmo remarked. The treat had completely numbed his tongue. This had never, ever happened, and, although it was inconvenient, he quite liked it. He licked at the warm air for a while, as if he were a panting dog, but then he went right back to eating. 'Ssllsmmsnnnmlllllmmm.' This was because he had never before encountered anything so delicious and also so much fun.

Once they had finished eating and Mary had crunched the cornet – which Lanmo thought sounded a bit like mouse bones – the snake lolled upside down from her shoulder, just holding on to her arm with his clever tail. He was so happy to have new things happen after such a long life and so happy to be with his friend and to see her so happy. 'Wibbibb wubbly.'

'I beg your pardon?'

'Ibbibb lubby.'

'Oh, Lanmo, your tongue has frozen.' And Mary giggled and the sound tasted of strawberries.

'Thifff iff lovely,' he managed and chuckled. 'I have freezy frozey tongue.'

'There's no such thing.'

'There must be. I have it.'

Lanmo could have spent all afternoon like this,

but he felt Mary turn and catch her breath as she looked up the avenue. Walking towards them he could see an almost familiar figure. 'That looks like Paul, only he is taller and older.'

Mary was waving at Paul, as if they had agreed to meet here. 'Of course he is taller and older. Time has passed.'

'Oh, but this is terrible.'

Paul was quite close now and Lanmo realised that letting his tongue get freezy frozen was a disaster. It might be hours before he could taste anyone properly. If Mary loved Paul and wanted perhaps to marry him, or go kayaking in the Arctic wastes with him, then the snake absolutely had to be able to taste him clearly and find out if he were reliable and if he loved Mary back and perhaps if he would be a good kayak paddler. Lanmo thought to himself, *this is what it must be like to be a human, to never really know or understand the inside of anyone else. And their eggs tell them nothing . . . They are poor, abandoned creatures.*

Because his tongue was of no use to him, the snake settled for staring very hard at Paul in an examining way.

'Ah. The snake is back.' And Paul looked almost angry as he continued, 'Snake, the last time you were here you bit Mary, and I have been told that you did not mean to, but I must tell you that if you bite her again then you will also have to bite me, because I will fight you.' And Paul's blue eyes shone very brightly in a brave way and his gingery hair became more ginger and he tried to stand so that he seemed big, even though he was still quite skinny and someone you would probably take for granted if you passed him in the street. That is, if you weren't Mary.

Mary – who *was* Mary – took Paul's arm on the side that was furthest from Lanmo and shushed him. 'No fighting. Please. I forbid it.'

Lanmo craned his neck (which was also his back and some of his middle) all the way along Mary's shoulders so that he could face Paul and say, 'If you fought me you would fight no one else, forever after.'

'I wouldn't mind. If Mary were safe I wouldn't mind a bit,' said Paul and, although his hands shook and his voice sounded wobbly, he stared into the snake's deep, deep eyes and didn't blink.

Then Lanmo nodded and winked and licked Paul's ear quickly with a slightly rubbery tongue and (while Paul squealed) the snake spoke to him in a voice like being hugged with warm towels after a long bath. 'You are a fine person, Paul. I think you will guard Mary almost as well as I could and, as I must travel a great deal about the world, you will have to do your best without me on some occasions.'

'I can look after myself, thank you,' said Mary, but she also squeezed Paul's hand so hard it nearly hurt him and kissed the one of his ears that Lanmo had not licked. 'We will look after each other.'

'Remember,' the snake told them as they strolled in the dusty old sunshine past the empty shops, 'remember that you must always lay your eggs in warm, dry sand, far from humans and their stupidity and angriness.'

Mary said nothing to this, only blushed. But Paul said quietly, 'I think perhaps human children do not require sand. Or laying eggs.'

The snake shook his head and thought how foolish the young pair were – they had a great deal to learn about parenthood. But perhaps they would have time to learn. 'I feel you might check that with a more experienced human to be sure,' he said. 'And now, Mary, you must tell Paul about adventuring and ask him whether he would enjoy sleeping in tents with spiders, or in caves with bats, or in jungles with panthers. And whether he would be able to wrestle a crocodile, or tickle a hippo, and all of the other things that any proper explorer has to do. Because if he is to spend his life with you then he will need to know about many such things.'

'He shall not at all wrestle any crocodile,' Mary told Lanmo. 'Don't tease him.'

'And I would rather not tickle a hippo,' nodded Paul. 'But I can light a fire with two pieces of wood and a bootlace. And I can find the North Star. And I have always wanted to go on adventures and swim beside whales and ride over prairies and—'

At this, he was interrupted by Mary kissing him on his mouth, because she was so delighted that they shared this large dream along with the so many other things they had in common. And he and she spun and spun in each other's arms until they were almost dancing along the uneven, grubby paving stones. Everyone who saw them never forgot how perfect Mary and Paul looked – two humans devoting themselves to each other in joy and tenderness. As the days to come descended, it was something to remember. When matters became grey, or hard, or uncertain there would often be a face in this or that crowd which was smiling slightly, thinking of the girl and her boy and their dancing and the light caught in their hair.

Of course, when Mary and Paul stopped dancing – although he loved dancing himself – the snake had gone.

And the snake passed, faster than threats or rumours, over the world. He met with many humans to do his work. He met a woman who loved the shape of bicycles leaning against walls and he met a boy who loved apples and a young woman who played the violin and who loved a young woman who played the flute and he met an old man who hated everyone he saw for reasons he told no one. And Lanmo sometimes met little girls, and they would remind him of Mary, and on those days, at the time when the snake knew it would be sunset in her country, Lanmo would send his friend especially wonderful dreams.

One evening, Lanmo met a man who was dancing. The sun in this particular land was slipping behind little, rounded hills and the long, rosy light it threw across the grass made the man seem taller and thinner than he was. His wife watched him from the kitchen window and loved him so much that the snake could feel it gathering in the grass like a stream of tickling water. And the radio in the kitchen pushed its music out into the air and the man danced and threw his arms over his head and danced even more. He looked like happiness.

The snake was about to open his mouth and show his teeth, but then, as he felt the tickle of the music and the tickle of the love, he began to dance instead. Between the man's stepping and shuffling and turning feet, the snake danced — hither and thither and to and fro. The snake wriggled on his belly — which he didn't often do — and shimmied on his back — which he never did. He balanced on his tail and swayed, he bobbed his head and closed his eyes, and felt, for a while, contented.

'Are you having fun?'

When Lanmo heard the voice, he opened his eyes and looked up. The man was standing still and studying him with a smile.

'You are an unusual fellow.'

Lanmo was strangely out of breath and had wanted to dance more, so he sounded whistly and slightly cross when he said, 'Yes, I am. You will never meet my like again.'

At this, the man frowned and sat down very quickly on the grass. 'Ah, I understand.' And he nodded very often and looked at the way the sun was dipping closer and closer to the hills as if it wanted to warm them very much. 'Yes, I see.' The man pulled his hand through his hair and then nodded again. 'I see.'

The snake should then have shown the man his teeth, but instead he smoothed along to sit on the man's knee and study him. It had been a long time since any human had noticed the snake and Lanmo had not spoken to a human since he had been with Mary.

The man gently rubbed the snake's neck. 'Well, my friend, I have thought of you often.'

'I am not exactly your friend,' said the snake.

'Well, my guest, then.'

Lanmo liked the gentle and sad way the man was touching his scales and found himself becoming drowsy. In fact, he fell asleep.

When he woke, he found he had been carried and coiled into a hollow that someone had made in some sweet, long grass left uncut to shelter wild flowers. It was not like him to sleep, especially when he was meeting a human, and he wondered if he were perhaps ill in some way. When he raised himself to look about, he saw that he was at the edge of the dancing man's lawn and that the man and his wife were dancing there together, their arms tight around each other, while music poured from their window and down into the closely clipped grass in that part of the garden. And a new taste of love raced between the blades of grass and the currents of the air as if everyone were under a waterfall. The love and music were both so thick now that the wife and the husband could only move very slowly. This was perhaps why the snake had been lulled to sleep – this excess of love and music.

Then the couple looked over towards the snake and saw he was watching them. 'We would prefer to be together,' said the wife and she put her hand over her husband's mouth so that he could not speak.

And the snake shook his head, because being together when the snake came for only one person was not allowed.

But the humans looked so sad.

'One of you has only a little time, the other has very much more.'

'We don't mind,' said the wife and she stared straight at Lanmo, because her love for her husband meant she could see the snake very clearly. 'I don't mind. You are a most beautiful snake and we are asking that you behave in a most beautiful manner. Please.'

Lanmo tasted the air and knew that what she said was true, that all of it was true. 'You would rather leave now?' he asked her.

'With my husband. Yes. I would rather not stay behind in a world with no colours and no music and no dancing any more. Which is the world it would become for me without him.'

The husband and wife looked at Lanmo. They held hands. And they waited.

And so the snake agreed they could leave together. But before that had to happen, Lanmo danced with them both until the sun set behind the hills and it was fully dark. Then, when the North Star was bright, he nodded to them, and everyone sat down on the grass, which remained warm with sunshine, love and dancing. And the snake let the wife and the husband meet him both together. While the couple held hands and looked up at the stars, the snake opened his mouth with his needle-sharp teeth that were as white as bones.

Afterwards, he slept in the hollow they had made for him in the grass, because this was the first home that had been built only for him. And when he woke he wept. This had never happened before and, because it was all so strange, Lanmo knew he must go and see Mary. He would ask her to explain.

When the snake returned to Mary's city he saw that, once again, much more time had passed than he had realised. There were no longer any kites flying over the rooftops. The streets were almost silent, apart from the barking of thin yellow dogs. The luxurious towers that had thrown their shadows over more and more of the neighbourhoods had been abandoned and become tall, thin ruins, or had been reduced to no more than rubble and foundations. It seemed that the hands of giants had reached down and punished them. The snake, because he was wise, knew that the hands of humans and the machines and devices of humans had caused the damage. Usually, this would not have concerned him. He had seen many cities and nations rise and fall. But this time, as he rushed to Mary's home, he discovered that he was terribly worried. He wished never to arrive but also to be in her garden already, pleasing her and making her laugh. He felt that he was being torn into two pieces and this made him think, *love truly is a terrible thing. And yet it makes lovers never want to leave each other and hold hands while they look at stars and be happy all the way to their ending. And that is wonderful. Love is strange.*

When he reached what had been Mary's house — far slower than he usually would have, because he was distracted — the snake found that the building had no windows any more and that none of its humans were still there. The snake's friend the kitten had also gone. The rooms in the tiny apartment were almost bare. Out in the garden the plants were growing as best they could without anybody to water and care for them. The roses looked tired and as if they missed Mary.

In Mary's room her bed remained, but without her blankets and sheets, or pillows. Resting on the bed were the embellished slippers that Mary had once been forced to make in her sewing class. They were placed neatly together on top of a folded note with 'FOR LANMO' written on it. The snake could read all the languages that ever were or could be and so he unfolded the paper and saw:

Dear Lanmo,

We have had to leave here and we do not
exactly know where we are going, so I cannot
tell you where you can find us. Even so, I really
would like you to find us, because you are my
best friend in all the world. Mother, Father,
Paul, Shade and I will start walking to the
north tomorrow where things are meant to be
better. (Except Shade will not be walking
because he only has quite little paws for
making a big journey. We are going to carry
him. He doesn't weigh very much, even though
he has grown up since you saw him last.)

Please do come and visit me if you can. I
know you are busy, but please do try.

And Paul says hello.

And thank you for the dreams.

And I am sending really all my love to you
apart from the love that is for Paul and
Mother and Father and the little bit I give to
Shade who is very sweet.

Your friend,
Mary

The snake tasted the letter and, even though the paper and ink were quite old, they still held the flavour of love. He closed his eyes for a moment and remembered lying on this same bed and looking into his friend Mary's eyes. The snake's heart had always been still throughout his thousands upon thousands of years of existence, but now it began, for the first time, to beat. The sound of it puzzled him.

He flickered his clever tongue into the air, so that he could taste exactly where Mary had gone to and then, faster than sadness, he made his way there. He moved too swiftly for anyone to see, but those humans he passed on his journey shivered and cried, or felt they must find those they loved at once and hold them and look at their faces with great attention and tell them kind and important things.

When the snake stopped his journey he found that he was by the side of a small path through woods. It was evening, and all around him the dipping sun showed signs that many people had passed this way. There were abandoned suitcases and empty food cans lying about, along with worn-out shoes. Next to a little stream someone had left a piano, having pushed it for many miles. The instrument leaned at a strange angle against a willow tree's trunk and when the wind blew the willow swayed and the piano's strings played their own small tune to the tree.

In the shadows under the branches of an oak, the snake saw a young woman with twenty-one white hairs and eyes that showed she was brave and kind and honest. She was wearing sturdy boots and sensible clothes that were cleverly sewn with tiny, strong stitches. She looked like someone who had always prepared herself to go travelling and to have adventures. But she did not look as if she were enjoying a pleasant journey. She seemed thin and tired and her boots were worn and dusty, as were her patched canvas trousers, and her shirt and coat were threadbare.

But the snake hardly noticed how Mary looked. (For the young woman was, of course, his friend.) He was in too much of a rush and too happy. 'Hello, Mary.' Lanmo flickered through the grass and sat on Mary's shoulder, resting his head against her cheek. He felt that his heart was beating very quickly and strangely inside him.

'Ah, Lanmo.' Mary stopped stirring a little pot of rice which she had hung over her cooking fire and began to tickle the snake's belly. The snake allowed this, even though it was a little undignified for so wonderful a snake as he. The tickling made him smile his almost invisible snaky smile and he realised that he had not smiled since he last was with his friend.

Resting at Mary's feet was Shade, who was now quite a grown-up cat. When he heard the snake's voice, he flicked his ears and then stood up and began pouncing and capering about, as if he could recall being a kitten and playing with Lanmo's tail.

'I knew you would find me,' said Mary. 'Paul said you would not be able to, but I knew you would.'

'And where is Paul?' asked Lanmo, worried that Paul had not been helping Mary on the journey, as he should.

Mary smiled. 'We passed a glade with mushrooms in it a while ago and I sent him to gather them now we have camped. I know from my books they are a kind that are good to eat. We can dry some for later and eat some now with this rice. He'll be back soon. And then it is his turn to make us a bed in the trees.'

'You sleep in the trees?'

'Of course. Where there are big trees we can climb, we always camp high up in the branches and keep away from any danger. And while I sleep Paul watches me and while Paul sleeps I watch him – in case we fall out and hurt ourselves. No one has to watch Shade because he is already very good at sleeping in trees. In fact, he has taught us a great deal about that. He is extremely wise for a small cat.'

Shade was standing with his front paws leaning against Mary so he could reach up and begin licking the end of Lanmo's tail and purring proudly. Lanmo permitted this, but when the cat gently nipped him, the snake had to give him a sharp look. 'I am not a toy,' he said. The cat did not entirely understand this; nevertheless he trotted away to look for something he might eat. The humans could not feed him any more, so he now had to hunt for himself.

For some time, the snake simply lay along Mary's shoulders and enjoyed her company. It had been such a while since he saw her. 'Time has passed,' he said.

'It has. It always does.' Mary nodded. 'We cannot stop it.'

He also flippery-flickered his tongue extremely fast so that he could learn about how many dusty and muddy and stony miles she had travelled and how sad she had often been.

When both our friends had closed their eyes and breathed a while and been content, Mary asked, 'Lanmo, have you met my parents?'

'They were not in your house when I visited there. Your letter said they had left with you.'

'They came with us as far as the edge of the city,

but then they said they were too tired and had brought too much to carry and would miss their home too much. And so they told us to go on without them. For three days and three nights, we camped together beside the ancient city wall and tried to change their minds, but every time we asked them to come with us, they refused. And when Paul and I and Shade woke up on the fourth day, we could not find them anywhere. They had left their parcels of food with us and a note that said they thought they would be too slow on the journey and would hold us back. And they left me this . . .' Mary showed Lanmo a golden chain which she wore around her neck. 'This was my mother's – she wore it on her wedding day.' And she had to wait for a while until she could speak again, because of the sadness in this. 'Paul and Shade and I looked but we could not find them. And how could they eat with no food? How would they do that? Why would they not come with me when I know all about exploring and journeys?' Lanmo felt his friend's tears drop onto his scales, heavy and stinging, with a strange new kind of love which turned his heart to an ache and made its beating stumble.

Mary's voice was very quiet when she asked, 'But it is your work to meet humans, isn't it? And once you have met them, they will have reached the end of their lives.' Her hand trembled against Lanmo's side.

'Well . . .' whispered the snake, 'that is true. I am sorry for it, I think. I never was sorry, but now I am. Still, a snake is a snake is a snake. And I am this kind of snake.'

'But you have never met my mother and father and let them see you and know your teeth?' Her voice was even quieter.

'I have not, Mary.' The snake nuzzled her cheek with his head. 'I saw them when I was with you in your house, but they did not see me. It was not their time to see me.'

And then Mary said no more, but Lanmo could taste that she wanted to ask him, 'And do you know if my parents are still in this world?'

So the snake tasted the air to see if he could find Mary's mother and father. His tongue searched in the air for a long time and would have gone on searching if Mary had not said, 'Lanmo, you cannot find them, can you?'

'No, I cannot.'

'And you have the cleverest tongue in the world, haven't you? And you can find anyone or anything?'

'That is true.'

'So if you cannot find them, then they cannot be

found any longer in the world. And humans have done your work for you.'

The snake did not answer this.

'I would rather not be human,' Mary said and she cried for a while and Lanmo cried with her. And this was the only time he had ever cried with a human.

Our two friends were simply sitting together quietly when Paul returned with the mushrooms. He was whistling merrily as he came along and doing his best to be happy that he had his gathering bag and all his pockets full of mushrooms. Mary leaped to her feet and hugged him, and Lanmo – who was riding on her shoulder – also enjoyed the hug.

Paul was startled to see the golden glimmer of the snake, but then he smiled and asked him, 'I suppose that you don't eat mushrooms or rice – and that is all we have to offer you.' He also whispered, 'I am doing my best to take care of Mary and she is doing her best to take care of me.' And then he shook Lanmo's tail in the way that a human might shake another human's hand.

Lanmo wasn't expecting this and it made him lose

his balance. For a while he found himself upside down and being shaken. 'Woo-hoo-oh.' But he quite liked the feelings this gave him and so he bounced up and down while Paul held him and chuckled. He had guessed that perhaps being silly for a while would cheer Mary up. And he was right.

Then Shade returned with a mouse. Although the snake was a little jealous of the cat's tender snack, he did not really need to eat to keep himself alive – it was only a habit that he sometimes enjoyed – and so he did not insist on sharing the furry little meal. He only looked at the cat with an upside-down look and said, 'There is a great deal of grass in the sky and the ground has become very blue and red with a sunset in it.' Shade put down his meal for a moment and licked Lanmo with a tongue that tasted of mouse. Lanmo chuckled again but then looked as serious as a snake can look and slipped out of Paul's hand and swung gently from a branch overhead.

After that, the cat ate its mouse and the humans ate their rice and mushrooms, and then Mary put out their fire very carefully so that it would show no smoke and they all climbed up high into the biggest tree they could find. From there they could see the lights of large fires and small fires, but mostly the land was in darkness. There were no lights from houses to be seen, even far away.

Lanmo said, 'You may all go to sleep tonight for the whole night because I will watch over you and keep you safe.'

This meant that Mary and Paul could snuggle together on a wide, old branch while Shade curled up by himself on a higher, smaller branch. Before she closed her eyes to sleep in her canvas sleeping sack, Lanmo slipped along in the dark to Mary, his wise eyes shining redly. 'I have never known a human like you.'

'Well, I have never known a snake like you.'

'That is true.' His red eyes blinked. 'The world has never known a night when I have not been passing from one land to another doing my work. But I will stay here and no one will meet me and no one will leave their life because of me – and this is for you.'

'Are you allowed to do that?' murmured Mary, who was feeling very comfortable because of having had such a good meal and was gently falling into all the good, warm dreams that Lanmo was already sending her to make her feel happy and refreshed. He was also sending Paul, who was already asleep, dreams about being useful and kind and attentive. And he gave Shade a dream about skipping up and down a huge mountain of cat food, chasing very slow, fat mice.

'I do not know if I am allowed to let all the humans live who would have left the world tonight. Perhaps they will have to stay in the world for a very long time as a result. But I do not mind. No one has ever told me what to do under these circumstances, because I think I was never supposed to have a friend and to understand love and . . .' Lanmo rested his thin, snaky chest against Mary's hand, 'my heart is beating.'

'Goodness,' said Mary, feeling the tiny *pitpatpitpat* of Lanmo's newly alive heart. 'I thought all this time that you had a beating heart like other snakes.'

'But I am not like other snakes.'

'Of course you're not. You are the only snake I will ever talk to and the only snake who will be my friend and the only snake I will ever love.'

At this, the snake cried a number of tears that were not unhappy. He had not known before that it is possible to cry because of joy. And then he sneezed – *pffs* – and tried to sound brisk, so that he did not seem overly sentimental. 'Tomorrow, you must stop going north and take the path that I will show you. You must go to the Land of Perditi where you will be safe. It is a long way, but you are a brave and resourceful explorer so you will reach it. Then you must go to the first city you reach after the mountains and you must take the roads as I direct you when you enter its gates and then you must knock on the house with the blue shutters and the blue door.'

'And will everything be all right then?'

'Everything will be as all right as it can be.'

'And will you visit me there?' For Mary already knew that Lanmo was going to leave again, because he was giving her so many instructions for the journey. 'I would like that.'

'And I would like that, too.' Lanmo snuggled under Mary's chin, just as he had when she was a little girl.

'Good night, my friend.'

'Good night, my friend.'

'Sweet dreams.'

'I have arranged that, yes.' And Lanmo lifted his head and kissed Mary's cheek and then was still.

And Mary did dream the whole of the journey that she must make, all night long, and when she woke Lanmo was doing his stretching and waking-dance, right along the branch just above her to make her smile.

'Oh, you are still here, Lanmo.'

'Yes. I will ride on your shoulder for the rest of the day and make sure that you have recalled your dream properly and then I must go and be busy in the world with the other humans.'

While Mary washed in the little stream not far away and filled their water bottles, Paul lit a fire – he was good at lighting fires – and heated some water for pine-needle tea. Then he washed, and Shade watched him splashing in the cold water and stubbing his toes on rocks. The cat just licked and licked his fur in the clever way that cats do when it is time for them to wash themselves. And Lanmo swung from the branches of the tree and his golden scales sparkled and he ruffled them so that the breeze made them sing and sound like better times and like a small orchestra, far away, walking to a party, or a wedding.

'Mary,' he asked when she sat by the fire with her pine-needle tea, 'have you married Paul?'

Mary shook her head. 'We wanted to get married, but then so many bad things happened that it was not possible.'

'I have the power to marry humans.'

This sounded not very possible to Mary. 'Are you sure?'

'Well, the captains of ships and all kinds of other humans may marry humans and humans are very silly, so I don't see why I can't marry you to each other much better than any of them. I am magnificent and wonderful and there is only one of me. Therefore . . . I shall marry you.' He paused and seemed to be making an effort to grin, in as far as this was possible. Certainly his scales bristled with excitement.

Then he wagged his tail to summon Paul and Shade closer, before hanging from a branch above them in a solemn manner. 'I hereby marry you. Shade?' The cat looked up at Lanmo's ruby eyes. 'You shall be our witness that these two are joined together in the ways that humans prefer.'

'But we have no ring,' said Paul, who hadn't quite expected to get married that day.

'And I was going to wear a remarkable dress and there was going to be feasting and music and . . .'

Everyone paused for Mary and no one said what she was thinking – that she had wanted her mother and father to be there. Each of them knew it, all the same. Paul – who had lived in an orphanage – might have invited some of the other orphans, but he had no idea where they were now.

Lanmo frowned and licked his tongue in the air with impatience. 'I cannot help any of that. I can only declare that you are married by all the power that is vested in me and that is a great deal of power.' He intentionally grew much larger and puffed out his throat like a cobra and glimmered impressively. 'And dresses . . . One can surely be married wearing nothing at all if one has to.'

Paul winced. 'It is not quite the usual way,' he said softly and held Mary's hand and kissed it. 'But we could be married and it would be wonderful . . . Oh, but we do need rings.'

'Very well,' said the snake. 'If you insist.' And he leaned over to Mary until he was almost touching her nose. 'Mary, you may pick two of my scales – the ones you think are prettiest – and then you must pull them out.'

'But won't that hurt you?'

'It may. I do not know. But they will each make a golden ring for you and for Paul. They will be rings like no other because you are humans like no other.'

And he closed his eyes and waited until Mary had indeed chosen two scales that seemed maybe a little smaller than the rest, so as not to hurt him, and pulled out one of them – which took all her strength. When she held the scale it was finer and thinner than the finest and thinnest silk but it weighed more than a heavy heart. Where the scale once was, a single drop of blood welled up and then rolled and fell, and when it touched Mary's hand for a moment it shone like a ruby and then it vanished into her skin. 'Oh, Lanmo. I am so sorry. This must be hurting you a lot.'

'I am being very brave. You may continue.'

And Mary pulled out another scale and another drop of blood fell and splashed onto Paul's forehead, and, near where it fell, twenty-one of his hairs changed to a bright golden colour, in amongst the red. This scale was also as thin as thin and very heavy.

Paul and Mary held one scale each.

Then Lanmo opened his eyes and gently kissed

Paul on the cheek. At this, the scale Paul was holding turned to liquid and flowed to form a ring on Paul's finger, a very beautiful ring, with its own tiny scales like a snake.

And next Lanmo kissed Mary. 'There, I have given you away, although you are not mine, but I do love you and so I have had care of you and now you are married.' And the scale she held then flowed from where it rested in her palm to form a shining ring on her finger, even more beautiful than Paul's, with a perfect image of Lanmo looped all around it.

Then the newly-weds and their cat and their friend the snake marched out on the first day of their journey on the snake's path and – as he had in happier days – Lanmo rode on Mary's shoulder, flickering his tongue and humming a small sweet tune to himself and occasionally sighing because he was so very comfortable and yet this comfort would soon come to an end.

When the humans had unpacked their gear and lit their fire for the evening, Lanmo told them, 'Now I have to leave you, but these rings will distract your enemies as you travel, should you meet any. Their eyes will be drawn to the gold and then they will feel sleepy and then they will be confused, and by the time they have recovered themselves you will have run far away.' He tickled the ears of Shade and the cat lay on its back for a while, remembering what it was like to live in a house and have nothing to do but eat and sleep and play games.

This looked so endearing that Mary and Paul watched the cat being happy. When they looked up, the snake was gone.

'Oh,' said Mary. And she shed a tear. The tear fell upon her ring and where it landed there grew a tiny diamond. And when another tear fell there grew another diamond. These formed the eyes of the snake that was imprinted in the gold. And this was a sign to show Lanmo that love is a jewel and helps us to see and is not only a terrible thing. Although it may also be a strange thing.

But Lanmo was not there to see it.

L anmo, with his newly beating heart, returned to his work, going up and down and around the world. He met woodcarvers and helicopter pilots and guitar players and swimmers and humans who wandered from place to place because they liked to and humans who wandered from place to place because they had no homes and humans who loved to whistle and others who loved to paddle and some who loved to climb trees. He also met humans who had never yet found anything, or anyone, to love. These humans made his heart beat slowly and grow heavy in his chest, and this disturbed him.

Every morning he licked the air with his wonderful tongue and tasted where Mary was and if she was happy. Every evening he sent her funny dreams and silly dreams and dreams where she won her heart's desire and dreams where she swam with tigers and then lay on the beach with them while their fur dried and they purred. He also, because he thought he should, sent quite pleasant dreams to Paul – ones where Paul was a famous footballer, or a beautiful giraffe, or a tree filled with parakeets. (Lanmo could taste that Paul loved football, giraffes and parakeets.) And the snake sent some smaller dreams about mice and biscuits and tickles to Shade. (Cats' dreams have to be small, because they need to fit inside catnaps, which are short.) And Lanmo made sure that all three of our friends knew where to go on the morning of each day when they woke.

And as he travelled across all the countries that humans have invented, Lanmo knew that on all sides the humans were performing his duties without him. It seemed strange to the snake that so many humans would use so many ingenious machines and so many ingenious excuses and so many ingenious methods to rush each other out of the world, when all of them must leave their lives in any case. *They should fly kites*, he thought. *They should play with cats and eat ice cream and bake bread and dance with each other and sing and they should marry each other and perhaps make intelligent children who understand things, or adopt children who are orphans and have nobody for them in the world.* But he knew

117

that he could not change the humans against their will and that the humans could only choose to change themselves and so he must leave them to be lost in their own ways.

Mary and Paul were not lost. For many months after they left their home city, they followed the dream map that Lanmo showed them, a little bit more every night. Their path was strange — it wriggled and squiggled and writhed and scrithed and did not include any straight lines in the way that a human path might. This was because snakes never move like humans and do not trust straight lines — they find them unnatural.

There were days when the path was dusty and our courageous three were thirsty by the end of the day, but the snake would make sure that by sunset they would find a stream, or a pool, or a well to drink from and a tree to climb, or a large bush to shelter under. And they would fill their water bottles once more and wash their faces and be glad. The travellers climbed into mountains so high that there was snow underfoot, but this didn't trouble them because Mary had packed them warm clothes and the snake would guide them to quiet corners in cliffs where they could huddle and stay warm and where they could find dry leaves and sticks that Paul could use to light a fire. Above all, the snake led them away from other humans, because this was a time when very many of the world's humans were too sad, or angry, or desperate to be safe. And when our three friends could not avoid humans, their rings kept them safe and they moved onwards.

This lack of other humans might have meant that Mary and Paul felt lonely, but in fact they were entirely content. They played with Shade and took turns carrying him when he was tired. They whistled while they trudged on and, as it happened, when one of them was weary and sad, the other was able to cheer them. They were never weary and sad at the same time.

And, one evening, they rested in bracken on a gentle slope that faced a beautiful sunset, as Lanmo had known it would. They had climbed over the highest of the mountains and that had been hard, but now they were descending and this was easy and they looked down at a wide and peaceful city where kites flew merrily in the breeze, perhaps a thousand bright red kites, bobbing and swinging and shining with red sunset light. (Lanmo knew about the kites and had – you will remember – told Mary she should stay in this, the first city after the mountains.) They had eaten some sweet berries they had never seen before and cooked some large roots which the snake had told them in a dream they should look for, dig up and then roast on their fire. They felt full for the first time in many months and this made them drowsy. (Lanmo had known this would happen.) Away to the east there was a high waterfall and the light through its water made rainbows that no one would have been able to look at without smiling. (Lanmo paused in his work while he knew this would be happening and he smiled his snaky smile and chuckled.)

So Mary was resting against Paul and smiling, and Paul was also smiling, and Shade was curled in Mary's lap and purring – which is a cat's way of smiling – and the birds sang and there was no sound of gunfire, even far away, and no sign of burning houses and no marching columns of men, or straggling columns of downhearted people. There was only peace. And suddenly Mary and Paul both had enough space in their heads to recall that they really were married and that they really did love each other and they held hands and they sang.

> *You are the night with sunshine*
> *You are the ocean with no shore*
> *You are the bird that sings wine*
> *You are the lion with no claw*
> *And be my honour and be mine*
> *And be my glory and be mine*
> *And be my living and be mine*
> *My friend, my love, be mine.*

And then they slept.

In the morning, they both walked down the slope, followed by Shade, who by now had turned into a rather larger, stronger and more impressive glossy black cat. Mary's twenty-one white hairs glimmered in the dawn light and, although her clothes (and Paul's) were faded and torn, today they both seemed somehow proud and calm and a little magnificent. Although they did not know it, a few days ago they had all crossed the border into the Land called Perditi, a country that Lanmo was sure would be safe for many, many human lifetimes.

As they neared the foot of the slope, they joined a smooth, well-kept road that curved towards a great walled city, held in a gentle valley. As they marched on, for the first time on the snake's path, our friends passed lots of other humans and even little stalls that sold cooked rice and meat wrapped in leaves. At first the sight of humans made them nervous and also ashamed because Mary and Paul knew they looked grubby and dishevelled. (Shade looked as neat as cats always do.) But the other humans nodded to them as they passed, or smiled, or greeted them in a language they could not understand, but which sounded friendly. A woman at a stall selling a kind of large red fruit saw how tired Mary and Paul looked and so she reached out her hands and offered them fruit. It had been a long time since either of our human friends had any money and so they shook their heads, even though the fruit looked delicious. But the woman just laughed and nodded and put one fruit into Mary's hand and one into Paul's and then waved them away. By signs and smiles — and suddenly feeling quite close to crying — Mary and her husband showed the woman that they were grateful. Then, as they marched on, they bit into the fruits and enjoyed the soft, moist, perfumed flesh which tasted a little like sunshine and a little like grapes. And, in the years ahead, they would always remember the taste of those fruits — which they learned were called *bamandaloo* — whenever they walked near the Wide and South Gate, which was the one they first used to enter the city.

The city was called Paracalon, as they later learned. It was perhaps not the most wonderful city in the world, but it was very, very good. When they entered Paracalon, they passed into the cosy shadows between three- and four-storey buildings with bright shutters and doors. There were small gardens and squares containing fountains, too, and Mary could hear singing from some of the windows. And above them flew the red kites.

Lanmo's dream had told them to take the left road when they came into the city and then the left road again and then the small road past the bakery on the right and then the lane on the left. At the end of the lane, which was lined with low houses and little gardens, was a house with friendly blue shutters and a friendly blue door. In the open doorway was a woman who had just picked some flowers from her garden to set on her kitchen table. When she saw Mary and Paul her face changed and her flowers fell to the path at her feet. 'Oh,' she said. 'For many months, I dream of seeing you both on my doorstep and I know that you should come, you should live. Here with me.' She had also understood from her dream that she should speak the language of the land

Mary and Paul had come from. She did so with difficulty and slowly, but they understood her.

Mary and Paul stood, dumbfounded.

'Really. Inside. Come. Breakfast.'

This seemed so strange and yet so wonderful that neither of our human friends could move, but Shade simply capered over the threshold of the house and lay in a patch of sun on the living-room floor, as if he had always lived in this house. He was a sensible cat.

As you will have guessed, the woman with the blue shutters was the good daughter of Granny Higginbottom. She was called Dora and she now earned her living by making jewellery in a workshop behind her house. She had been able to begin her business using the precious jewels and metals Lanmo had brought her and now she was looking to take on extra help. Her husband, Peter, was busy woodcutting some of the time and busy looking after their grandchildren the rest of the time. He was not very good at making jewellery, although he was otherwise very nice. Lanmo had sent Mary and Paul to exactly the place where they could be useful and happy. Dora had wondered what new rings she could make, but when she saw Mary and Paul's rings, she knew that they should all work at making snake rings. And so they did, learning as they went along.

In the end Mary and Paul became very fine jewellers and also learned to speak the language of their new home very well. And, although the rings the humans made were not as delightful and graceful and magnificent as the ones the snake had created from his scales, they were still quite lovely and sought after. And Mary also invented a way to make necklaces like the one her mother had given her, so long ago.

After this, as with all grown-ups, Mary became very busy with her good, full life. She and Paul had no children, which made them slightly sad because they had wanted to raise a little boy and call him Lanmo and teach him to climb trees. But sometimes what we want does not happen, even if we want it very much. Still, Mary and Paul were like an aunt and an uncle to Dora and Peter's grandchildren and, in a way, they became one very large and joyful family together, with outings and festivals and dancing and songs. And above the house they flew a red kite, which Mary discovered was a sign that whoever lived there had survived a great journey and was alive and well.

Each evening the kites waved and bowed to each other and said in their own languages, 'Hurrah! We are alive! We are happy!'

And in this being busy, Mary did not exactly forget the snake, but sometimes she did not think of him very much. Also, she had not seen him since her wedding and she had begun to think that he would not visit her again. Each night, he sent her beautiful dreams and sometimes she would hear his voice in them, chuckling or boasting, but when she woke he would not be resting on her pillow, or licking her ear with his tongue.

And, of course, time passed.

And then, of course, one particular day Mary was walking in what was now her garden in Paracalon — a place with rose bushes and a seat beneath a tree. By this time her twenty-one white hairs were impossible to see, because all her hairs were white. She was standing looking at the kites, free in the blue, blue sky and thinking that to love something did not mean that she could own it. She had loved Shade very much and yet, in time, he had left the world. She could not keep him. She had loved Paul very much and yet, in time, he had left the world. She could not keep him. Since Dora's children had moved away, Mary was the only human in the house with the friendly blue door and blue shutters. And the snake that she loved so much must have come to call there many times but she had not seen him, or heard him, because loving him did not make him appear when she wanted. This made her sad, even though she understood that she and Shade, Paul, Dora and Peter had lived very long and wonderful, lucky and marvellous lives.

Still, these thoughts were making her a little sad when she felt a tickle at her ankle and looked down to see a glimmer of gold and the blink of two red eyes. 'Mary, you have changed.'

'I have grown old, Lanmo.' She smiled and watched as the snake sleeked upwards until he was sitting neatly in her palm, just as handsome and proud as he ever was, for the snake never did change. 'Time has passed.'

'Well . . .' The snake flickered his tongue. 'I did not quite mean to be away so long.' Then he climbed quickly to sit on her shoulder and whispered in her ear, 'I am so glad to see you.' And he looked at the two little diamonds that shone in Mary's ring — the diamonds that were once tears — and they told Lanmo so very much about love that for a moment he held his breath.

Seeing Lanmo made Mary feel almost as if she were a young girl again and that soon it would be time for school and that somehow she would walk into a room somewhere and her parents would be sitting there with a table set for dinner. 'And I am so glad to see you.' She turned and kissed his elegant golden head – something that no other human being would ever be permitted to do. 'Hello. And thank you.'

'Oh, I did nothing really.' The snake might almost have been blushing, if it were not impossible for snakes to blush. He rustled his scales so that they sounded like the waves on a wonderful shore far away. 'Hardly anything.'

'You saved my life. And Paul's. And Shade's.'

Then there was a pause and a silence that glistened like molten gold and sunsets and furnaces. It felt like diamonds.

The snake spoke again to Mary, in his softest and gentlest voice. 'I never save lives.' And these were the saddest words he had ever tasted.

'You are wrong.' Mary shook her head and smiled. 'You saved us.'

Then she went and sat under the tree that gave a good view of the mountain range she had climbed over so many years ago with Paul and Shade to find peace. The snake kissed her cheek and sighed. 'Ah, Mary. You are my best friend. You are my only friend in all the world.'

At this, the friends nodded and were silent.

Then the snake kissed her again, once on her forehead and once on her hand, just where his tooth had brushed her. Then he slipped down into the grass and lay like a resting bolt of lightning.

Mary told him, 'I always wanted to make a bangle that looked half as beautiful as you, one that shimmered and glimmered.'

The snake blinked and raised his head and Mary could see that he was crying and could say nothing more.

She said, 'But I think that I have no more time to try.'

And the snake she called Lanmo waited in the grass for her to come and meet him. But when she stood and took a step, he cried out, 'No. No, Mary. You must remember that when you take very tiny steps the garden will grow and grow. Take only the very tiniest steps.'

But then she took another step and he called out, 'No. No, Mary. You must take much smaller steps than that.'

But then she took another step and he called out, 'No. No, Mary. You must remember that if you take no more steps then the garden will go on for ever and ever and will not end and nothing will end, not any more, not ever. Please.' And that was the first time the snake had said please. 'Please.' And that was the second time. 'Please.'

And that was the last time the snake ever said please.

And what happened next I cannot tell you. No one can make me.

So this is almost, but not quite, the whole of the story of how a snake's heart learned to beat. And this is almost, but not quite, the whole of the story about a remarkable, wise little girl called Mary and the friend that she called Lanmo. And this is almost, but not quite, the whole of the story of something wonderful and terrible and strange.

And it may be that Mary and Lanmo are waiting with each other in the garden to this day. I know they both would have liked that.

Acknowledgements

With thanks to Hans Koch and
Antoine de Saint-Exupéry.

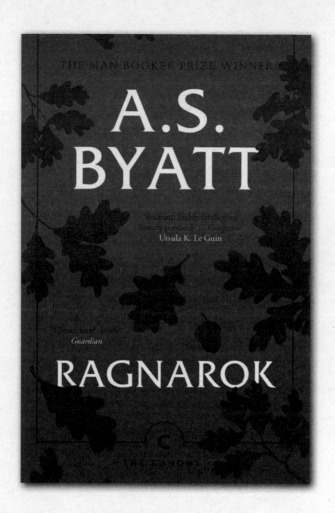

A.S. BYATT

'Brilliant; highly intelligent,
fiercely personal . . . Gorgeous'
Ursula K. Le Guin

'Clever, hard, lovely'
Guardian

RAGNAROK

THE CANONS

'Byatt's prose is majestic'
Sunday Telegraph

CANON GATE

Natsuo Kirino

THE GODDESS CHRONICLE

Daring and disturbing *Los Angeles Times*

'One of the most unexpected and playful novels to
emerge from Japan in recent years' *Telegraph*

CANON‖GATE

AUTHOR OF ORANGES ARE NOT THE ONLY FRUIT

Jeanette Winterson

'Playful, expansive and full of heart'
The Times

'A masterpiece'
Scotland on Sunday

Weight

· THE CANONS ·

'Profound and provocative'
Daily Mail

CANON▌▌GATE